PICTURE
THE DEAD

Adele Griffin AND Lisa Brown

PRAISE FOR PICTURE THE DEAD

"A tour de force, a remarkable feat of visual and verbal story-telling, as playful as it is serious, as haunting as it is delightful."
—Michael Chabon, Pulitzer Prize-winning novelist

"Don't believe in ghosts? Read this book. Adele Griffin delivers an atmosphere of creeping menace while exploring the many sides of devotion to the living and the dead. Lisa Brown's illustrations, which incorporate drawings, letters, lists, clippings and dance cards, are beautifully twined into the text, reminding us that all mysteries—even unearthly ones—are solved by an accumulation of fact, memory, and the instinct for the telling detail."
—Judy Blundell, author of *What I Saw and How I Lied*, 2008 National Book Award Winner

"I loved *Picture the Dead*. Eerie, romantic, moody, and immersive. A beautifully illustrated gothic delight!"
—Holly Black, *New York Times* bestselling author of *Tithe: A Modern Faerie Tale*

"Open *Picture the Dead* by Adele Griffin and Lisa Brown and step into a rich, nineteenth-century scrapbook filled with ghosts, betrayals, murder, and love. A haunting work, beautifully told."
—Brian Selznick, Caldecott Medal winner and *New York Times* bestselling author of *The Invention of Hugo Cabret*

"Love story, mystery, ghost story...*Picture the Dead* is a gripping, gorgeously graphic novel about a girl who risks everything... Jennie's voice and the pictures she shows us bring this swift, wonderfully chilling story to life."
—Kit Reed, author of *The Night Children*

PICTURE THE DEAD

ADELE GRIFFIN
and
LISA BROWN

SCHOLASTIC INC.
New York Toronto London Auckland
Sydney Mexico City New Delhi Hong Kong

ISBN 978-0-545-34349-7

12 11 10 9 8 7 6 5 4 3 2 1   11 12 13 14 15 16/0

Printed in the U.S.A.   23

This edition first printing, September 2011

Internal illustrations by Lisa Brown
Cover design by The Book Designers

Lexile is a registered trademark of MetaMetrics, Inc.

I HAVE NO FEAR OF PHOTOGRAPHY AS LONG AS IT
CANNOT BE USED IN HEAVEN AND IN HELL.

—EDVARD MUNCH (1863–1944)

Toby —
my twin,
my alter.

Stevensburg Virginia March the 20th 1864

Mr. Henry S. Pritchett
Brookline Mass

Dear Sir,

It is with the utmost regret that we inform you of the death of your nephew, Tobias Pritchett Lovell of Captain James Fleming's 28th Massachusetts Infantry, Company B. Private Lovell died not on the battlefield, but on his sickbed & was none the braver for it I he bore his painful illness with Fortitude & strength of Spirit, fighting as hard as any true Christian Soldier sacrificing his Life for his Country.

I will now endeavor to give you the Particulars of his Death, as far as I am privy to them. Pvt. Lovell fell ill with Dysentery on March the 15th, and was removed to the Hospital at Stevensburg on March the 17th, where he was treated with kindness & concern. Every measure was taken to secure his Health & were confident of success. Sadly, on Marc unexpectedly worsened &

Mr. Henry Pritchett
Brookline, Massachusetts

THE
UNION
FOR
EVER

J.M. WHITTEMORE & CO., 114 WASHINGTON ST., BOSTON

STEVENSBURG
APR
4

1 CENT

1.

A ghost will find his way home.

It's dark outside, an elsewhere hour between midnight and dawn. I lie awake, frozen, waiting for a sound not yet audible. My eyes are open before I hear the wheels of the carriage at the bottom of the drive.

And now the dog is barking, and there's faint light through my window. The hired man has emerged from his room above the stable, lantern swinging from his hand. I hear Uncle Henry's lumbering tread, Aunt Clara's petulant "Henry? Who is it, Henry, at this hour?"

I know that the servants are awake, too, though I can't hear them. They have been trained to move in silence.

What if the carriage brings news of Quinn and William? Or even my cousins themselves? That would be too much luck, perhaps, but I'm not sure that I'm strong enough for less. Another loss would be unendurable. And we are never given more than we can bear, are we?

When I sit up, I am pinpricked in fear.

The corridor is freezing cold, and the banister is spiky, garlanded in fresh pine. With both sons at war and her only nephew buried this year, Aunt Clara nonetheless insisted on bedecking Pritchett House for the Christmas holiday. Uncle Henry always defers to his wife's fancies. She's a spoiled child, blown up into a monster.

Downstairs the front doors are flung open. I join the household gathered on the porch—all of us but the hired man, who stands below in the drive as the trap pulls up. The moment feels eternal. I twist at my ring, a diamond set between two red garnets, more costly than the sum of everything I own. When Will slid it onto my finger, he'd promised that I'd get accustomed to it. Not true, not yet.

"Doctor Perkins," says Mavis, raising the lantern as the doctor jumps down from the buckboard. The housemaid's chattering lips are as blue as her bare feet, and her braid swings so close I could reach out and yank it like a bell cord if she didn't scare so easy.

The doctor signals for Uncle Henry to help him with another passenger.

Quinn. The name shatters through me.

Aunt Clara looks sharp in my direction. Had I spoken out loud? I must have. But I'm sure it's Quinn. And as the figure emerges, I see that I'm right.

Quinn. Not Will.

He is grotesquely thin and hollowed out, his left eye wrapped in a belt of cloth that winds around his head. He is barely human.

"I'll need hot water and clean bandaging." Doctor Perkins is speaking as Mavis's lantern pitches, throwing wild shadows. "A step at a time, Henry."

On the sight of her favorite son, Aunt Clara whimpers. Her hands clasp together under a chin that wobbles like aspic. "Oh, my darling boy, safe at home at last."

Quinn ignores her, an old and useful habit. He brushes past Aunt, the plank of one long arm hooked over Uncle Henry's neck. But then he squares me in his eye, and in one look I know the worst.

Will is not coming back.

Blood rushes to my head; I might faint. I lean back against a pillar and take slow sips of air.

"A few more steps," pants the doctor. "Where is the closest bed?"

Quinn's bedroom is all the way up on the third floor, an inconvenient sickroom. He'd moved there last year, before he'd found a richer rebellion in joining the army and leaving home altogether.

"Give him Jennie's room," says Aunt Clara. "Go on. It's only one flight, off the landing. And Jennie can sleep up in Quinn's room. It will work perfectly."

These suggestions part so quick from her lips that I know they've been squirreled in her head for a while. Even through her dread and worry, my aunt has been plotting against me.

A very bad sign.

2.

Mavis has darted ahead. Before the others have a chance to tromp their boots through my bedroom, she has rushed in and collected my treasures. Father's pocket watch, my brother's and my christening cups, the lace collar I have been straining my eyes and fingers over these empty evenings. But most important is my scrapbook. I shudder to think of Aunt Clara's fat fingers picking through its pages. Perched on top of my possessions, in an offering of solidarity, is a photograph of Mavis, plain as a platter in her Sunday best. I will add it to my book when I have more than a moment to myself.

The room is tiny and airless and fitted with a narrow bed, an iron nightstand, and one dreary dormer window. Quinn had called it his rookery, and he'd relished its perch high above the family. I don't feel the same way.

I exchange my candle for Toby's little silver cup, and I wedge myself into the windowsill, bumping my head on the eave. My temples pound, my lips are dry, my mouth tastes of ash. I stare out at the tar black sky.

"Toby," I whisper. "Is he with you?"

In answer, silence. But I know I'm not alone. A ghost will find his way home. I learned this nine months ago when my brother died in a field hospital in Stevensburg, Virginia. I was in the parlor that day, using the last light to cut linen strips for the Boston Ladies' Aid. Toby's presence was a wave crashing over me, knocking the breath from my body. Three days later we received the letter.

Many people have asked me if it's strange to be a twin. I'd say it is far more peculiar to be a single twin. I was Toby's alter and his double, and we created shelters for each other in the physical world. In life he'd been shy, and his death before he'd seen a day of combat was a quiet end to an innocent young life.

And yet in death Toby isn't ready to go, or to let me go. We used to predict our futures on scraps of paper in the downstairs coat cupboard. When I stare into the eyes of his photograph, which is safely tucked inside my scrapbook, I can hear his whisper in my head, confiding his dreams to spy for the Union and regaling me with stories of Nathan Hale and how wars are won through ciphers and invisible ink. "A spy sees everyone, but is seen by no one," he loved to say. "Remember that, Jennie."

Other times, like now, he keeps silent, but I sense him. He guards me in spirit just he as did in the physical world. He has brought me closer to the other side, and I know that I'm changed.

"Please, a tiny sign," I whisper, my hands clasping the cup like a chalice, "if Will is really dead and gone."

"Who's there?" Mavis has rushed into the room with armloads of my clothing. Her gaze jumps around the darkest corners of the room.

"Nobody. I was…praying," I fib, hiding the cup from sight, and then we're both self-conscious. Mavis makes a business of hanging my dresses in the single cupboard and folding some of my personal items into its top drawer. As I pace the room, worrying the frayed sleeve of my dressing gown between my fingers, I catch sight of myself in the window's dark reflection. My hair springs wild from my head, and there is a stunned look in my eyes, as if I am not quite available to receive the news that I'm dreading to hear.

"Quinn is settled?" I ask.

She smothers a yawn and nods. "Doctor Perkins sent him to bed with a grain of morphine. Everyone says it's rest he needs most, but oh, Miss Jennie, he's got so thin, hasn't he? Just the bones of his old self."

"I think Will is gone forever."

"Now, why would you say such a thing?" Mavis genuflects, then points the same finger on me, accusing. "Like you *know* something."

I hadn't meant to say such a thing. I hadn't meant to speak at all.

"But you're awful cold, Miss." She catches my hand and squeezes, as though it's she who frightened me, and not the other way around. "I'll build up a fire." She drops to kneel before the grate, steepling nubs of kindling. "And I'll fetch you the rest of your clothing come morning," she murmurs, "though you *ought* to be downstairs in the yellow room." She strikes the match and sits back on her heels as the flame catches.

"Aunt Clara'd have given me the yellow room if I'd asked for it." The hour is late, and I'm drained, but Mavis is a delicate soul, led often to fears and tears. "It'll be pleasant roosting up here near you. Nobody to pester us."

She attempts a smile. "Not Missus Sullivan, anyways. She sleeps like the dead, specially if she'd nipped into the cooking sherry. You'll hear the mice, too. They get ornery when they're hungry." She waves off the phosphorus and steps back to watch the fire crackle. "I'm awful sorry, Miss. It pains me. This room's not fit for the lady of the house."

"I'm not the lady of this house."

"Soon you will be, and everyone knows it. He'll come back to you. By the New Year, I'll predict." She's predicting a miracle.

I look down, and my fingers find my ring, which twinkles in the firelight like an extravagant and sentimental hope.

My tears will come later, I'm sure. Right now, I don't want to believe it. I want to wake up from it.

U. S. Military Telegraph.

May 7th, 1864 186

Chancellorville, Va. 186

By Telegraph from Mr. Henry Pritchett

To Mr. Henry Pritchett .... Brookline, Mass.

It is with deepest regret that I inform you of the death of Corporal Pritchett, killed in line of duty in the Wilderness. He put up a brilliant fight.

My Sincerest Condolences,
Captain James Fleming,
28th Infantry Company B.

Dahlias
Lovely Child

Toby

Charlie

Will, dead all these months —
Yet so alive in his letters.

Will and Quinn, 10 years ago —
in those days, as inseparable as a
thumb from its print.

Helleborus
I brought some
of these to Quinn —
don't think he
noticed

3

I wake with a pit in my stomach. I wish I could yank up my quilts and hide from the day, but the morning doesn't know to mourn. The winter sun smiles over my view of the kitchen garden. Hannibal struts the fence, sounding his imperious crow. Aunt Clara's clipped holly bushes are interspersed with hellebores, all blooming in obedient array.

I'll bring Quinn some flowers. An innocent excuse to pay him a not-so-innocent visit, but I need to hear him say it out loud. Of the two brothers, Quinn was more often the subject of Toby's and my whispered confidences. We were cowed by his coolly impeccable demeanor and hurt by his ice-pick wit. Will was easier—either warmly, sweetly happy or in a hot temper. Nothing in between, nothing to hide.

"Even if Quinn thinks we're low and unschooled," Toby once declared, "I wish he'd do a better job of pretending he didn't." As we got older, we avoided our cousin rather than shrivel under his scorn.

Quinn's bedroom door is shut. I hesitate as my eyes land on a photograph hanging in the corridor. It had been commissioned of the brothers last spring, and in their summer suits they make quite a pair. Aunt enjoyed celebrating her handsome sons, both of whom she swore had the Emory chin, the Emory nose—if pressed, she would avow that Quinn and Will possessed the Emory everything, with Uncle Henry offering scant more than his surname.

I tap. And then again. Even when I creak open the door, Quinn doesn't turn. He lies in bed like a prince on his tomb. His bandages are an unwieldy crown. But he's awake. I jump to hear him speak my name.

"Yes," I tell him. "I'm here."

"You hate me, don't you?" he says without looking at me.

I am startled that my cousin would care what I think. "Don't be ridiculous." I place the vase so he can see it. The morning light is stark. I can barely recognize my returned cousin. Mavis was right—he is a living skeleton.

"Mrs. Sullivan says it might snow later today. But it appears that Mavis has already stocked enough firewood to keep you warm." I add another birch log to the fire, but the chill has seeped inside my bones.

"You wished I were Will. Last night I could see it in your face. You wished he'd come home instead of me." He scowls. "Mother's joy doesn't make up for your devastation."

"No, you can't—"

"And why wouldn't you mourn? My brother was your beloved, and now I'm your enemy—even if you'll never admit it. I convinced him to sign up with the Twenty-eighth, and I failed my most important duty, to bring him back alive."

"He's gone, then." I force him to confirm it. "He's been killed."

"Yes."

I'd been braced for this truth, but I'm not sure I ever would have been prepared for it. The air leaves my lungs. It takes all my resilience to walk across the room and slip my hand into Quinn's. He is suffering, too, after all.

His palms are calloused, chapped. Gentleman's hands no more. "Quinn, tell me. How did it happen? I'm strong enough to stand it."

"If I'm strong enough to tell it." He swallows. "Undo my bandage first. And bring me a mirror. I want to see my eye."

"But Doctor Perkins—"

His head jerks up from the pillow. "If it were your eye, you'd snap your fingers for a mirror and command me not to bully you."

Quinn hasn't lost his uncanny ability to pin me to my own logic, but I'm too weak to spar with him. I retrieve the hand mirror from the bureau. Then I sit close and begin the odious task of unwinding his bandages. My attention is grave and utter, and for a few minutes there's no other sound than our breathing.

I thought I'd been ready, but a scream fills the cavity of my body as I peel back the last blood-crusted layer and let the cloth fall from my fingers.

In the flinted symmetry of his face, Quinn's wound is monstrous. Bruise-blackened, his eyelid raw as bitten plum, the whites of his eye filled with blood. He takes the mirror and stares at himself, then puts it down and looks at me, his head tilted like a hawk. Quinn was so beautiful. How he must suffer this mutilation. I pinch my thigh through my skirts as I return his gaze.

"It must have been terrifying to be shot," I say. The tremble in my voice betrays me. I sense his dare for me to keep looking.

"It was, but this wound's not from gunfire. It was Will who took the bullet." Quinn's words are hammered flat, though there's density of emotion behind them. "That's all you want to hear about anyway. On May sixth. It pierced his lung. We'd been fighting in Virginia, southeast of where we lost Toby. A special pocket of hell called the Wilderness." His hand slips under his pillow and pulls out an envelope, thin as a moth wing.

I open it. The paper of the telegram is creased and blotchy, but the writing is legible enough to see what matters. The message is signed by a Captain James Fleming.

I refold it and return it to Quinn, vowing to come back for it later. I'm not stealing; I need it for my scrapbook. It's evidence, a dossier fit for the spy that Toby had so desperately wanted to become. In the months since his death, I've been honing my skills. Toby was an astute observer. He never got lost; he could see like a hawk. Now it is up to me to adapt these habits. If I'd been his brother instead of his sister, I'd have stepped firm into Toby's boots and charged out the door in a heartbeat to join the infantry, becoming the Union scout he wanted to be.

But this telegram, which I'll tuck alongside Will's dog-eared letters home, are mostly evidence of a life cut too short. I hold my spine straight. The least I can do is not break down in Quinn's presence when he's had to carry the burden of this news.

Still, my mind is spinning back through time. My last letter from Will had been postmarked the third of May. He has been dead all these months. How could I not have sensed it? How could I be so vain as to presume that I would have? Inexplicably, I'm furious with my twin. Why does Toby shadow me if he can't serve as a messenger between worlds?

"Was he in terrible pain?"

"Not so much as shock."

"And you were with him in the end? Or did he die alone?"

"I was with him. Of that I can attest."

"Did he...did he have any last words?" *For me*, I add, silently. I feel tears and blink them back.

"He went pretty quick, Jennie."

"What of his things? Things he carried—" I'm thinking of the necklace that I'd given to Will before he'd left, a silver chain and heart-shaped locket, inside which his miniature faced mine. Will had promised that he'd wear it next to his skin every day and that, dead or alive, the locket and chain would one day return to me. But I don't quite dare speak of it particularly, lest Quinn think me even more selfish than he already does, utterly absorbed in my own loss.

"I've got nothing," he says. "Other soldiers stole us blind before we'd got to the Wilderness...our watches, my belt buckle, my spurs. It happens. We all joined up so dumb and green, nobody thought... nobody expected—" His voice breaks off.

On impulse, I reach out and smooth his hair, gingery brown and long enough to curl around his ears. It's uncommonly soft, like kitten fur. I don't think I've ever touched him before. His skin burns under my fingers, as though with fever. Quinn flinches but doesn't move out of reach.

"There's a new kind of quiet in this house," he says softly. "It bothered me all last night. It kept me up, and when I did sleep, I dreamed myself back into other times, like last Christmas. Remember last Christmas, Jennie? The four of us together skating on Jamaica Pond, and all our cracking-fun snowball fights, and how we carved our initials in the bark of that butternut tree?"

I smile. "Of course." The memories warm me like a sip of brandy in an ice storm. "And you're right. It's been too quiet here. And so

lonely," I confess. "I've missed you—all of you—a thousand different times a day. All of these months with only Aunt and Uncle have been enough to drive me mad."

Suddenly Quinn's hand wraps hard around my wrist. He grips me tight, his bones shifting around mine. I wince, but he won't let me go. "Jennie, promise not to listen to gossip."

"What gossip?" His hand doesn't loosen. Fear holds me in place. "What do you mean? Is there something else I need to hear? Because I'd rather it come from you than the servants."

"Only what I've said. War changed us. We always meant to be decent. We meant to do right. The dead cannot defend themselves, but surely they have paid enough."

"Of course," I murmur.

He releases me, but Quinn has a secret he's not telling.

The dead cannot defend themselves. It's hard to imagine William Pritchett being less than absolutely decent, or doing anything that he needed to explain. Boisterous, spirited Will, who loved nothing better than camping and fishing and sleeping under the stars, was tailor-made for military life. Could he have changed so much?

"Don't say anything to Mother. Let me be the one to give her the news."

"She's not a fool. She and Uncle Henry know as much by what you haven't said."

Quinn nods. "Send her up as soon as soon as she's ready."

I nod, but Quinn's eyes are closed again. He has dismissed me.

Aunt Clara
She is MONSTROUS.
I HATE her

Uncle Henry

Suzanna Pritchett Lovell and Matthew Horne Lovell
"Mother"   "Father"
1824 – 1859   1819 – 1861

4.

"Goodness. If I didn't know better, Jennie, I'd think you suffer from club foot." Aunt Clara doesn't take her eyes off her toast. Her delicate jet earrings tremble as her knife scratches at the toast like a cat's paw, buttering every inch. Strange how even the most mundane habits of dislikable people can strike such harsh chords. I even hate the way Aunt *butters*.

"I'm sorry, Aunt." I tiptoe to my chair. It's all I can do to keep up a pretense of normalcy. The idea of food and polite conversation is very nearly unendurable.

Will is gone. Will is gone.

"Don't be sorry to me. It's Quinn you'll wake." Her eyes are silver, like a wolf. They are Quinn's eyes, but cruel.

"He's already awake," I return. "I took him some blooms from the garden." I unfold my napkin as Mrs. Sullivan bustles through the dining room with the sausage and eggs and offers the tray to Uncle Henry. The yolks of the eggs glare at me. I swallow the bile in the back of my throat.

"Perchance your billy goat's trot is even more effective than Hannibal's wake-up call." Aunt poses it as a witticism, but I feel the lash of her thought. I've never been Aunt Clara's ideal speci-men of niece, with my flat feet and too-curly black hair and wide-lipped laugh—though there's been no reason for laughter these past months, and certainly not this morning.

Aunt Clara has alternately thrown her thunderbolts of disdain and rained down her indifference on me from the day Toby and I arrived at her door, nearly four years ago. Uncle Henry's half sister's orphaned children. Not only were we barely blood relations from the bottom of the social heap, but we were willful youngsters at that, prone to speaking without thinking and doing without asking per-mission. If it hadn't been for our doting eldest cousin, Aunt probably would have turned us away within that first month.

"He wants to see you after breakfast, Aunt," I say. "He has some-thing to tell you."

She nods, but her lips sink and her face goes pale. "That was my intention."

"He's asked me to tend to him regularly, though. As his nurse."

"Nonsense," says Aunt Clara, with a sweep of the jam spoon. "That's a mother's duty."

Uncle Henry rubs at the back of his balding head, his overused signal that he is uneasy with the friction in the room. Neither Aunt nor I pay him any attention.

"He was very specific," I insist, my words racing out quicker than my understanding of them. I am lying, but *a spy must embrace the unex-pected.* If I don't put myself to good use, I'll have no reason to be here at Pritchett House, and Aunt Clara would like nothing better than to pounce on this point.

After all, I am sixteen years old, nearly grown, my school days finished, my fiancé dead on the battlefield, my future as valuable as a wooden nickel. Death tolls are delivered with the paper every morning, and it's not as if I haven't imagined this dark hour. I need Quinn as never before. He's Aunt's favorite, her baby boy, but Aunt doesn't have the patience to nurse him— or for that matter, anyone—to health. If I care for him with diligence, or so I tell myself, the family's gratitude will keep me here until I find a better plan. But if I'm ahead of Aunt Clara, it is only by a step.

"Absurd," she mutters, almost as an afterthought, but then she's silent.

Perhaps this is our last breakfast together. Once Quinn shows her the letter, Aunt Clara might take to her bed, her antidote to the unexpected. Days could pass without a glimpse of her. Possibly she will become deranged, and Uncle Henry will pack her off for an extended stay at Taunton, the state lunatic hospital.

It could happen. In the years that I have lived under the Pritchett roof, I've witnessed Aunt's sulks and tantrums, her mood shifts from shrieking laughter to boiling rage, followed by withdrawal. Yet her resentment of me is a constant foul weather. It is little help that I resent her right back. In my scrapbook I've taken out my anger on her picture, knowing she'd never pull her bulk up the stairs to snoop through my possessions.

In the baleful silence, I watch her chew her toast, taking her time. Deliberate, controlled, delaying what waits for her upstairs. No, she would never indulge herself even the briefest lapse of real sanity. Not while I am under this roof.

If anyone is in danger of being packed off, it is I.

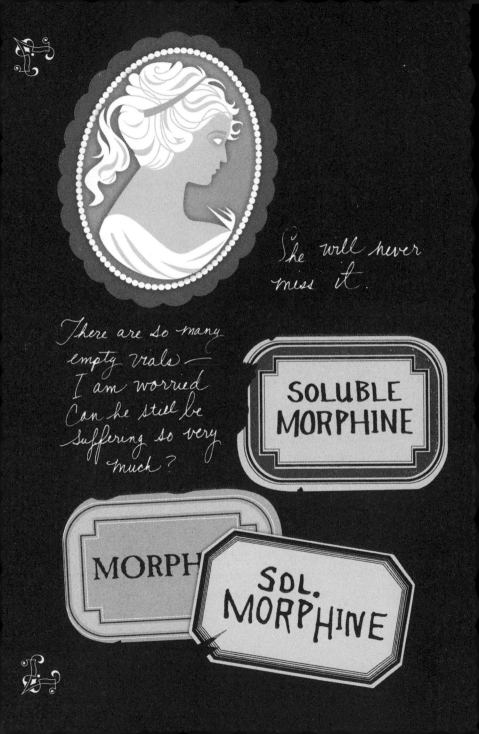

She will never miss it.

There are so many empty vials — I am worried. Can he still be suffering so very much?

SOLUBLE MORPHINE

MORPH

SOL. MORPHINE

5.

Will is dead. The days are interminable. Uncle Henry uses business as his escape, and he takes the carriage to Boston nearly every morning. Aunt refuses to leave her room. She won't see visitors and accepts only tea and holiday fruitcake brought to her door by a twice-outraged Mrs. Sullivan, who thinks liquor in cakes is a sin and that food in bed brings mice.

Quinn may be his mother's favorite, but she is far too lazy to commit herself to the daily duties of his care. I move in quickly. Bustling about him, serving or clearing or tidying up, my hands are never idle.

I yearn to ask him more about Will, but Quinn makes conversation nearly impossible. Clearly he prefers his books and privacy to anyone's company, and when I arrive with fresh pitchers of water or bowls of soup or clutches of firewood, he exchanges only the barest pleasantries, and always in a voice that suggests he'd prefer our chats to be as brief as possible. But this is how he's always been—save last winter, when he'd stolen a kiss behind the pantry door, his breath sweet with mulled wine, his silver eyes sparkling with mischief as his hands made a vice round my waist.

"Twenty-one inches, I wager." His words wet in my ear, and I was sure he'd have moved for a handful of my bottom next if I hadn't wrenched away, too shocked to speak. I'd never mentioned the incident, neither to his brother nor mine, and I was sure he'd long forgotten it.

"He is still so arrogant," I whisper to Toby's sympathetic silence.

But that's not quite true. Quinn is different. His sleeping is fitful, and more than a few times I've entered his bedroom presuming he was deep in conversation with Uncle Henry, only to find him quite alone and talking to himself. When he does leave his room, it's always without warning, and always many hours after the house has retired, to roam outside. Empty bottles of morphine are strewn on the floor beneath his bed. His strange behavior isn't lost on the others.

"I do think Quinn's gone off his head a bit, Miss," Mavis confesses.

"He's in mourning. We all are."

She curls her lip, unconvinced. "He's reliving his battles in his head. Many's the night I spied him through my window wandering the garden, cursing and shouting. The day girl's seen him, too."

"He's in pain. When the morphine subsides, it makes him wakeful." Outwardly I shrug it off, though I, too, have stood in moonlight at my dormer, watching Quinn pace the garden border.

"Missus Sullivan says she's got a mind to give him a talking-to, what with all the cursing. Not to mention the mud he tracks through the house," Mavis continues. "But she doesn't know the half of it. At night, when he's up and about, he goes and hangs blankets over the mirrors—not just in his room, but in the hallway, the parlor. I yank 'em off in the mornings when I'm lighting the grates. It's the right thing to do, isn't it?"

I nod. "It is. And you mustn't speak of it either, Mavis. Quinn's health is nobody's business but our own."

In her too-hasty nod, I sense Mavis has told her sister, Betsey, who is the Wortley family's cook. "Why'd he cover the mirror, d'you think, Miss?"

"He doesn't like to see his face, with his eye so badly wounded," I guess. "We'll have to be patient. It will take a while for his eye to heal." I can tell that my answer leaves Mavis unsatisfied.

My old friends at Putterham School would look down their noses at my intimacy with Mavis, but I take comfort in her company the same way I take warmth by the kitchen hearth, where I'm rescued by practical tasks. There is no place in wartime for a lady of leisure, and the kitchen is Pritchett House's hub of information. *A spy can move in any slipstream.* Scrubbing parsnips or peeling carrots, listening to the odd wag from the delivery boy, eavesdropping on the hired man's ribald jokes or recounts of his exploits at The Black Eye—his tavern of choice—I can loosen the hinges on my troubles. I collect gossip in much the same way I collect items for my scrapbook: warily, delicately, and with great care that I am not observed.

The kitchen is no place for a lady, but surely I am better off here than upstairs scribbling in my diary, pacing the halls, staring into mirrors or out windows and half listening to ghosts, and waiting all the while with a worried heart for Quinn to rouse and turn his cold stare on me.

"You ought to go comfort Missus Pritchett," Mavis had implored one afternoon, passing me on the scullery steps. I'd looked up from my task, scaling cod for a chowder, the fish lumped in my apron and the scraps pail wedged between my ankles. "You both loved Mister William. Let it draw you together instead of apart." Her bony hand had briefly squeezed my shoulder. "You got no business down here. You go remind those Pritchetts that you're still *family*."

She was warning me. Yet I couldn't muster the energy to tend to my aunt. The few times I had, I'd hated every moment.

"You're lucky, you know," she'd decreed bitterly as I arranged the silver service to her liking and poured her first cup of peppermint tea.

"How is that, Aunt?"

"You don't know the intensity of a mother's love." Her eyes were baleful, her pudgy finger crooked.

"I loved him, too, Aunt Clara." I moved away to re-swaddle the bed iron so that I wouldn't have to look at her.

"Yes, in your own, childlike way. But not profoundly."

It would be so easy to agree. But I despised her for discounting my grief, and it surely showed in my face. How could it not?

Next time, I let Mavis take care of the tea service, stopping in just long enough for an obsequious curtsy and to slip a brooch from the top of her dresser into my pocket. I didn't trust myself not to hold the iron too close to her toes, or to upend her tea in her lap.

Family, indeed.

On Christmas Day, however, Mavis's warning comes back to sting. We've left Quinn behind to attend church. It is my first outing since his return.

At least it's a diversion. I feel unfamiliar to myself—a secret widow in a starched black dress. I stare out the rocking carriage, with its passing convergent view of Jamaica Pond now in steely winter freeze.

Uncle Henry and Aunt Clara sit side by side and in hushed voices decide on a service for Will. It will be a sort of funeral, body or none, with selected hymns and readings. All planned for sometime after the spring thaw.

As I try to catch bits of talk, it dawns on me that Aunt Clara hasn't once consulted my opinion on these arrangements.

As if to emphasize this point, as we turn up the churchyard gates, Aunt jerks forward, her palm outstretched. "Why, Jennie, you are still wearing your engagement ring!" she exclaims. "Of all preposterous sights. Give it here at once, before anyone in the congregation sees it on your finger."

"Clara, dear," says Uncle Henry. "Now is hardly the time."

"That ring is no longer hers to wear. It is a Pritchett heirloom. Unless one is a nun, one cannot be engaged to…a spirit."

"Yes, of course, but…" Uncle Henry lapses off, astonished, as always, by Aunt's vile outburst but unable to find the words to refute her. He rubs the back of his head.

"Will was far too sentimental," Aunt continues, daubing her eyes. "Any adult can see this for what it was—a fickle vow from a boy too young for marriage to a girl too giddy to know better."

"He loved me," I whisper. "And that ring belonged to Grandmother Pritchett. Surely I can keep it?"

Nobody answers. The silence has hard corners.

Aunt Clara is wrapped head to toe in crepe so stiff she appears almost inhuman. She is a lump of coal in the corner of the carriage, her outstretched hand insistent as a beggar maid. If Will were here, we'd have been able to laugh at her. Alone, I find her quite terrifying.

The ring catches on the net of my glove and grips the bone of my finger. I wince as I pull it off. Aunt snaps the ring into her purse.

"I have Will's favorite hymn," I murmur in Uncle Henry's direction. I think of it, written out in Will's fine script, pressed into my scrapbook with a lock of his hair. "He would have wished it sung for him. At the service."

But Uncle will not look at me.

William and Quincy —
rescued from
Quinn's fit of temper

6.

"Then what did she do?" Rosemary's quick breath frosts the air.

"After screaming like a banshee and running up and down the stairs? She pulled the pine garlands off the banister, " I recall. "And she ordered the hired man to take away the Christmas tree and the ivy wreaths." I've been saving up this story and am probably too satisfied with the shock in the girls' faces, though it's all true.

Besides, the Wortley sisters—indeed, all of Brookline—must have heard some version of how Aunt Clara first took the news of Will's death.

"Mrs. Pritchett's got a boiling-hot temper." Flora shakes her head in dismay. "She would have been a fright to behold."

Christmas service is over. The familiar faces in the pews, the flickering candles in the stained-glass windows, the timeworn story of the baby in his crèche, and the hot cider and gingerbread in the long room afterward have given me a small and temporary peace.

Arm in arm, Flora, Rosemary, and I now walk the pebbled pathway that winds down to the Walnut Street Cemetery. My hands hold a single poinsettia, stealthily broken off the altar arrangement, to place on Toby's grave.

Aunt Clara and Uncle Henry linger near the vestry, consulting with Reverend Meeks, but I don't want to hear Aunt insisting that Will's service is given proper fanfare. Especially when Toby was buried in the same pine box he came home in and Aunt wore black for less than a month.

"Poor Mrs. Pritchett," murmurs Rosemary. "To bury a son. Not that it isn't deeply affecting for you, Jennie, only you're so young and sweet. Love will find you again. But Mrs. Pritchett is past forty. She has nothing to look forward to but the grave."

"She has venom in her yet. She took back the ring Will gave me."

"Nooo…" Flora's primmed face reminds me of when, in our last year at Putterham School, we'd stuck a clothespin on her nose to try to straighten it last minute, before the end-of-year class portrait.

"She wrenched it off my finger. She nearly drew blood," I embellish. "She despises me because she thought Father was common and Mother a heathen to marry him. Aunt Clara is a hideous, beastly thing." After all these weeks of being shut in that house, my words huff like an engine whistle pitched high and strong.

Too high, too strong. In fact, Rosemary has broken her link through my elbow and drops pace so that our skirts no longer swish in tandem. "She *is* your guardian," she murmurs, both arms crossed in the clutch of her Bible to her bosom. Flora's teeth gnaw her thin bottom lip.

I have overstepped. These girls like to gossip but are easily cowed. Quickly I change the subject. "Is there news of your brother?"

The sisters' words tumble over each other. "Silas is well—"

"And stationed in Franklin, Tennessee—"

"Quite far from the fray!"

Twenty minutes ago the congregation was voicing prayers for

the Godspeed return of all our soldiers. My resentment of Silas Wortley's safety is positively unchristian. "Well," I say, fixing a smile to my face. "Thank heaven."

"But tell us, Jennie. We hear from the servants that poor Quinn's gone…off," says Flora. "That he talks to himself and hides the family portraits, and that he roams the garden at unearthly hours!"

"They say he is addicted to opium…and that it makes him quite mad," adds Rosemary, with a smug flourish.

"All nonsense." I scoff, even as I feel my cheeks redden. "Quinn walks 'round the garden three times a day on the doctor's orders, because he needs the fresh air. And yes, we've hung some crepe over the mirrors. Just like any other house in mourning. But I suppose that's how these silly stories get started."

The Wortleys nod, seeming to accept this, but I'll have to speak with Mavis about being more careful about what she says to Betsey.

Because some of what they say is true. Only two days ago Quinn tore down the portrait of himself and Will that hung in the hall and flung it across the room, cracking the frame and smashing a wall sconce beyond repair. Nobody has dared to rehang it, and so I have wedged the damaged frame into the back of the guest room armoire and pasted the photograph in my book for safekeeping.

Rosemary speaks in a burst. "What are you going to do, Jennie, dear? Without Will to marry you, Mrs. Pritchett might just snap her fingers and force—"

"Hush, Rosemary!" Flora's eyes shoot daggers at her younger sister. "I'm sure Mrs. Pritchett would never dare. Let's speak of pleasanter things."

I hesitate, then plunge. "Might I pay a call to your family next week?" A despairing edge grates my voice and embarrasses me, but I press on. "Say, Tuesday? I'd be so glad to steal away for a few hours."

"Oh. Lovely." But Rosemary gives care to her next words. "If you could arrange your carriage to arrive by half past two? For that's when we'll be finished with dinner."

I am mute with mortification. Both girls know that Aunt Clara would never permit me use of the carriage for my own amusement. In the pause neither sister offers use of the Wortley coach—yet of course they'd be priggishly aghast if I arrived at their doorstep, my hem muddy from walking.

"Or…if you don't mind waiting until after the New Year for a visit, Jennie? Right now's the height of the season. Simple as we're keeping things, what with our boys away, we've got so many fittings and invitations. It's been such a flurry," Flora reminds.

Debutante season—I'd forgotten. Of course, I am not coming out. Nor shall I assume the enviable role of the newly affianced, with all of its attendant teas, dinners, and parties. I am trapped at that house until such a day as Aunt sees fit to cast me off. My future is at the mercy of Aunt's whim, and there's not a soul in Brookline who doesn't know it.

As tedious as it is to be pitied, it is positively frightening to be shunned. Worst of all, though, is to be forgotten. I must find a way to rescue myself. If there is only one thing I am certain of, it's that.

Amelia Rose Pritchett May 1855 - February 1857
Baby Amelia, rest her soul. Who would she
be today? The spitting image of her hateful
mother? Or a cushion against her attacks?

Private Séance by Miss Fanny Conant,
OF BOSTON
Admit...... *Miss Rosemary Wortley*..........
to private Séance on. *Monday August 16*........
at. *7.45*.o'clock p.m. prompt,
to be held out... *Mrs. Edward Olmsted.*
High Street Hill. please make no inquiries
THIS TICKET NOT TRANSFERABLE

Darling Will, ever the scholar.
(And yet not an hour after this oh-so-serious
portrait, we'd run down to the pond, bare
toes in the long grass.)

Rosemary gets all the fun. Wish I could have been there, too.
I would give ANYTHING to see Elizabeth Barrett Browning.
I wonder if she's VERY beautiful?

7.

The Christmas rain lulls my scrambled mind to sleep. It is still sluicing when I'm jolted awake, gagging, panicked, unable to breathe.

The thin chain of my necklace is wound like whipcord around my throat. I clutch at it and hear a whisper fast in my ear. A rush of words just outside my reach.

"Stop it! Stop!"

I kick and thrash, struggling against the stranglehold, but it's as if invisible hands clamp a vice round my neck. The whispering intensifies. The words seem purposefully distorted. I can't make any sense of them. All I know is I need to get out of this room at once. Coughing, fighting to breathe, pulling up from the bed, unable even to see my own hands in front of my face, I stumble to the door, yanking it open, and I run into darkness.

At the landing I stop, bending double, heaving wretched gasps as my hands lock my knees. My throat feels crushed, my breath so dry it pains my lungs.

"Another nightmare," I whisper hoarsely. My eyes roam, adjusting to pick out the outline of the furniture down the corridor— the slipper chair, the console. "That's all." That whispering was no more than the hum of my own pulse. And that necklace is long lost, strewn and trampled into some bloody Southern field, or tucked into the fat purse of a grave robber.

This lingering sensation of being watched hangs heavy on me. My toes and fingertips are ice, my heart is pounding. But I won't return to my bedroom. Not just yet.

I hasten down the corridor and the stairs. On the second floor, I follow the weak bar of light under the library door. I peek in. Uncle Henry is slumped in his armchair, staring into the dying embers. His decanter of whiskey is nearly finished. The flickering light scoops dark hollows into his eyes.

"Uncle?" I open the door.

His gaze shifts in my direction. "Amelia?" For a moment I'm confused, and then I remember.

"No, Uncle," I say quickly. "It's only Jennie."

Little Amelia was Uncle's and Aunt Clara's daughter, who would have been nearly my age had she lived past her fragile cradle years. Once last summer, when Tobias and I were playing spies in the garden, we'd overheard Aunt and Uncle speaking of their phantom daughter as if Amelia had never died.

"It's a game," Toby had said, "to give themselves comfort."

"A horrid, morbid game," I'd asserted as we'd sprung like a pair of frightened grasshoppers back to the safety of the house.

"Jennie, your niece," I prompt, for Uncle's expression frightens me. Everything in me wants to turn my heel and run. Instead, I venture into the room.

Uncle has gained weight. His chin folds like dough over his neck, and his buttons strain his waistcoat. He is holding out Amelia's memento mori. I suppress a shiver. Images of the dead provide not an ounce of comfort for me. The body present, stiff as an unlit candle, with the soul extracted from it.

"Jennie, yes. Come in." No, not Amelia's last image, which I had folded into my book years ago with a delicious shudder, but a tintype of Will taken last year, to commemorate his acceptance to Harvard. He'd been there only a few months, though, before yielding to Quinn's belief that one shouldn't hide from military duty.

I take the print hungrily and resolve to add it to my collection once Uncle Henry is out at his office. Will looks so alive that I cannot believe he isn't anymore. I remember precisely the expression on his face when he used to kiss me, the way his eyes had searched mine, those lips on my skin, his fingers tracing the outline of my chin and neck, sketching my body. Even the memories can turn my insides molten.

Uncle Henry breaks my concentration. "Jennie, I am obliged to ask a favor of you."

"Yes, Uncle?" I wait, vulnerable. At the mercy of whatever this request might be.

"A delicate matter." He reaches for his drink, his fingers clumsy. "So delicate, in fact, that I cannot make inquiries at the bank, or even the club."

I nod as he drains the glass, though this couldn't be good news. What sort of task would be beneath Uncle Henry but proper for his sixteen-year-old niece?

"There is a photographer in Boston. Not the usual sort, this gentleman. He goes by the name Geist," says Uncle. "He claims that he can conjure images of the departed. A medium, I think he is called."

Photographing spirits. "I've heard of this." From Rosemary Wortley, actually. She is fascinated by séances and likes to show off her invitation to a meeting she attended last summer while visiting

47

her Milford cousins. Where, she claimed, she had helped to raise the turbulent soul of Elizabeth Barrett Browning. Why would Uncle want to speak with me about such a matter?

"Quite. And I suppose that your father, my late brother-in-law, with all his daft ideas, might have had his hand in something like this. Didn't he have some like-minded cronies who all gathered at that church on Irving Street?" Uncle strokes his bald patch and continues. "Jennie, with your late father's connections, I'd like you to make some further inquiries."

"I'm afraid I don't understand." Although I am quite sure that I do.

Uncle turns and squashes my hand into his. His palm is damp, his eyes bulge with entreaty. "For God's sake, listen to me, girl. Imagine if Mrs. Pritchett and I could glimpse our son again. Or commune with his spirit, just once more, before we die!"

For all of Aunt Clara's caterwauling, I suppose I hadn't given much thought to how Uncle Henry has been affected by the loss of his eldest child. Certainly Uncle was always puzzled by Will, whose tender warmth stood in contrast to both parents' stylized graces. But Uncle never struck me as the sort to keep company with Spiritualists. Did he and Aunt Clara devise this plan together?

In the pause, Uncle Henry's fingers tighten, pulling me so close I smell the whiskey on his breath. "We have suffered so much already. And we have been kind to you, haven't we, Jennie? Frankly, I think it is the least you could do while you remain here at Pritchett House, reaping the benefits of our hospitality."

Heaven above, he is threatening me.

Spiritualists have no place in upper-class, conservative society. Possibly, neither do I. And so I am the correct choice for this matter.

"Yes, Uncle," I say. "I will do what I can. I promise."

Tobias and me, September 1848

a WEAK CHIN IS THE SIGN OF A TRAITER.

A SPY Must no When and How to terN to STONE

January the fourth, 1865

Dear Miss Lovell,

Thank you for your delicate inquiry. It is to your utmost commendation that you appear to be approaching this endeavor with your mind open to Spiritual Possibilities.

I would be delighted to accommodate your family at my studio between the hours of ten and eleven in the morning on Tuesday January the eighteenth. Please be advised that the greater number of family members in attendance could certainly improve the efficacy of the process. In addition, the presence of an object belonging to or depicting the beloved departed might encourage an Apparition.

But be forewarned: Services will be Promptly rendered, but with no Assurance of Spiritual Communication.

The summoning of Spirits is neither simple nore _____

skills _____

Josep_____

Your _____

Hein_____

Trem_____

HEINRICH GEIST
MEDIUM AND PHOTOGRAPHER
Tremont Street
Boston, Massachusetts

MEDIUM • PHOTOGRAPHER
HEINRICH GEIST
Tremont Street
Boston, Massachusetts

8.

Heinrich Geist is a large, bewhiskered man, younger and stouter than I'd imagined. Under caterpillar eyebrows, his eyes are blunt as bullets. I imagine those eyes staring at us now through his camera lens, and a chill creeps up the back of my neck.

Crammed onto one side of the gravy-brown love seat in Geist's sunlit parlor, which serves as his studio, with the perfume of Aunt Clara's oiled ringlets sticky in the air, I wish I'd had a bite to eat this morning. But I'd simply been too nervous. I was ten years old the last time I sat for a formal photograph. Even now I can almost feel the press of Toby's hand slipped into mine, for comfort.

"Chin up," he'd told me. "A weak chin is the sign of a traitor."

"Another minute," commands Geist, his voice muffled under the drop cloth.

I hold my chin high.

Standing behind me, Quinn exhales through his nostrils, signaling his displeasure.

Today is January the eighteenth in the new year of 1865. "A significant date," Geist had assured us as he'd ushered us into his sunny parlor, "for communing with our departed."

Quinn had snorted at that, too.

"Your folly surprises me," my cousin had rebuked when I'd first approached him. "Photographers are opportunists. Like cockroaches on the battlefield, scurrying for their capital on the dead. A boy's face for sale to his grieving family makes a tidy profit."

"Mr. Geist is more than a photographer. He is a medium." I'd shown Quinn the business card Geist had enclosed with his reply to my letter. "And Father's friends at the Swedenborgian church aren't charlatans—they were kind to me when I asked about Mr. Geist. I'm sure he'll be a gentleman as well."

"Perhaps." Quinn's lips had tightened to signal his doubt. "But most mediums are frauds who'd steal the pennies off a dead man's eyes."

"Yet the movement has believers," I'd insisted. "And Mr. Geist writes in his letter that the more family I bring, the better our luck. Come with us, please?"

"It's nonsense that Mother and Father agreed to such claptrap. But I'll do it for you, Jennie. Know that." His silver eyes had been steady on mine, and in a tingling moment I knew that Quinn hadn't forgotten that kiss after all.

Blushing, I'd dropped my eyes to study the laces on my shoes. "Thank you, Cousin."

In the end, I rationalized, he'd probably relented only to relieve his boredom. There are only so many trips around a garden that a young man can make. I hoped it was a good sign that Quinn was looking to become more sociable again.

My own reservations have more to do with money. Five dollars seems like an extravagance for a single portrait seating, and Geist had requested that we pay five more when we are delivered a photograph. I can't help but think of the warm winter cloak, new hat, and boots I could have enjoyed for the same price.

Services will be Promptly rendered, but with no Assurance of Spiritual Communication, Geist had clarified in his letter.

But this first attempt at *spiritual communication* is anything but otherworldly. My eyes itch, while my face is stiff as a cold caramel. Only a few minutes have gone by, but it feels like an eternity.

"Persevere, family," Geist intones. "William Pritchett is close at hand."

Will has never seemed so far away. He'd laugh to see us now. How fascinated he'd be with Geist's instrument and tripod. What amusement he'd take in Aunt, who holds one of his Harvard photographs balanced upright on her plump knees.

According to Geist, the photograph provides passage for Will's spirit to enter this gathering of Aunt Clara, Uncle Henry, Quinn, and me. "The deceased are drawn to their loved ones like butterflies to sugar water. Our beloved often appear to us through vapor or mist," Geist had clarified. "Other times, another passed soul—such as an angel or a Native Indian—is sent to serve as messenger."

This had provoked a dramatic gasp from Aunt Clara, who has a fondness for angels.

Now Geist jumps out from under the muslin drape and darts around to the front of the camera.

"Oh, dear. Is something broken?" squeaks Aunt through gritted teeth.

"Not at all." Geist fits the cap on the lens then slides a rectangular plate into the body of the instrument. "Exposure to the light is crucial to our success. But now we're finished. I have cut the light. The butterfly is in the net, so to speak. You are free to move. I feel certain that

William Pritchett was with us! Did you sense it?" His eyes rove the room as if following a starling. Then he slips behind the camera and removes a wooden box, the same dimensions of the plate, from its body.

Geist then hands the contraption to his waiting housemaid, who scurries off with it at once.

"A most confounded thing," declares Uncle Henry, "but I experienced a tickling in my fingers."

"A chill down my neck, perhaps," Aunt Clara whispers.

"What rot." Quinn sighs. His suit bags at the seams, but a faint glow of health in his cheeks offsets his auburn hair, and he has traded his bandages for an eye patch, which I privately think makes him look rather rakish.

"And you, Miss Lovell?" The photographer folds his black-tipped fingers over his chest and rolls back on his heels. Judging by my imploring letter, Geist must think I'm the most susceptible of us all.

I incline my head politely and say nothing.

The maid reappears in the parlor door. She is a plain thing. Buck-toothed and as jumpy as India rubber. "Dinner's in the sitting room."

"Thank you, Viviette," says Geist. "And now, if you'll excuse me to my darkroom." He takes swift leave through the parlor.

"Absurd," Aunt Clara mutters. "*Viviette.*" She mistrusts servants who sport exotic names. She thinks it makes them sound wanton.

Eyes averted, the maid leads us to a sitting room cluttered with bric-a-brac. My father once said that the character of a household can be known through the behavior of its staff. I don't know what to conclude from Viviette's refusal to meet my gaze.

The sandwiches and cakes are stale, the tea too strong, and the tables and walls are blanketed in photographs of vistas and monuments—my eyes are caught by a daguerreotype of Big Ben, the largest clock in London, which I yearn to see. There are also several portraits of Geist himself and stacks of *cartes de visite* of Geist and of his maid, modeling evening dress, street clothes, and even swathed in Grecian garb. Stealthily, I slip a few into my pocket.

"He watches us, even in his absence." Quinn rolls his eyes, and we trade a humorous glance.

Silence holds the room until the spiritualist returns. There's a bounce in his step. "Promising, promising! Now we wait until the varnish has dried and the photograph is printed. Then we shall see the fruits of our labors."

With no mind to his blackened hands, Geist helps himself to sandwiches and tea before launching into a fascinating recount of his youth in Paris.

"I studied under the esteemed photographer Monsieur Disderi. Odd fellow but brilliant. Disderi made his money in his portraits of the upper classes, such as the present emperor, Napoleon, who considers him to have procured his very best likenesses. But Disderi will also go to great lengths to authenticate rumors of spirit activity. Why, that gentleman once stood sentinel for twenty-four hours at the Place de la Republique in order to photograph Marie Antoinette's ghost on the scaffold, in her mobcap and with her hands bound."

"How did he…when did he…?" A crumb trembles on Aunt's lip.

"There'd been sightings every October sixteenth, the anniversary of her death. Doubters dismissed these as hearsay. Disderi proved them wrong. One glimpse of this image of the last queen of France would turn your hair stone gray. But that is nothing on Disderi's journey to Scotland and his singular images of pagan spirits who have haunted Tulloch Castle since the twelfth century."

Geist's anecdotes are so captivating that eventually even Quinn leans forward in his chair.

"I want to travel the Continent," he confesses.

"Go first to the City of Light," says Geist. "Fill your mind with beauty." He jumps up to leave the room and returns with a stack of tintypes. "Locke ought to have stayed there. He's destroyed his sanity. But his images will bear witness to this war long after we are departed." Geist hands them around for us to examine.

I examine portrait images of young boys with guns high as their chests. Rows of the dying. Rows of hospital beds. A look at Quinn, and I can tell that each image has hit him as a punch.

The pictures have a dizzying effect on me, too. I'm not sure if I'm mesmerized or daydreaming, but the heat is with me all at once as my memory catapults me back to last year, a languid August afternoon. Will and I had strayed from our picnic spot to go boating, and a boy, watching us push off from the bank, had decided to rifle through the belongings we had left behind, including Will's sketchbook. Ripping out the pages…yes, I remember…the little troublemaker had then set them afloat in the water, and Will had blazed with fury. I'd never seen him in such a temper, and it had taken him the rest of the day to calm himself.

My eyes are staring into Will's eyes—black irises ringed in pale blue.

I open my eyes and Will stands before me in blazing life in his Union uniform. The bottoms of his trousers are wet, and water darkly pools the carpet. His anger is palpable. He is so real, so alive, that I can inhale the tang of the salt water that he has carried in with him. If I reached forward, I could ball my fingers in the rough broadcloth of his jacket, my mouth could find that secret space where the carved notch of his collarbone met his throat and—

"Miss Lovell!"

Everyone is looking at me.

I blink. Will is gone. I am slumped in my chair, my teacup has fallen, and its liquid has soaked the carpet.

Quinn has left his chair and is bent on one knee before me. "Jennie?" he whispers softly. "What's the matter?"

"Nothing." I sit up. "I'm sorry."

"Miss Lovell, are you unwell?" asks Geist.

"No, no, I'm sorry—excuse me, I need air." Quinn helps me to stand, but his hand, gripping bony at my elbow, is no comfort. I shrug him off, but then I am embarrassed, my palms lifted in protest for anyone to follow. I am careful not to look at Aunt Clara as I hasten out.

Alone in the hall, I untie my collar and fan my cheeks with my fingers. Though my fever ebbs, I have little doubt.

Will was here. He was in this house, in that room, if only for a moment. But it was as true a moment as I have ever lived.

On the front hall table rests a small, paper-wrapped package, twine-tied, inscribed with the name *Harding*. The package is approximately the same size as the plates Geist had inserted and removed from his camera.

A good spy is never afraid to transgress.

I look over my shoulder. Nobody is in the hall.

My heart could take wing, it's beating so fast as my fingers unpick the twine. The knot gives too slowly. Then I slide a series of identical photos from their wrapping.

Backed and framed in a cardboard slip, a man sits as grim as a tombstone on the same ornate love seat of Geist's parlor. Above him hovers a delicate, nearly transparent image. Dressed in gauze, a crown of holly leaves twisted through her pale, streaming hair, the angel appears otherworldly and is more exquisite than my most vivid imaginings.

For a moment I am struck paralyzed. Here is a real angel, caught and captured in all her radiant glory, for anyone to see.

Incredible, but true.

I hold it up to the fanlight for a closer look. There is something familiar in the angel's profile. I decide to take one of the copies, sliding it into my pocket with the rest of my day's loot before the family comes to collect me. I compose myself, avoiding Quinn's eye, my own gaze intent on Aunt Clara's enormous, bustling skirts.

In the carriage, when I dare to look across at Quinn, he ignores me with a cool indifference that makes me miss his brother all the more. How is it that Will—even in spectral vision, if that's what it was—can appear more vital and vibrant to me than anyone else in the family?

I don't look up again for the rest of the ride home, lest anyone see my suffering, which the Pritchetts would only dismiss as a weakness.

In my attic room the light is weak. I move to the window and spread my secreted photograph on the sill. White winter sky exposes the image. And now I can see the slight protrusion of the angel's front teeth. I retrieve the other photos from my pocket.

The drape of Viviette's Grecian toga makes a lovely angel's cloak. I find the downcast eyes, that droplet nose, the bird bones of the neck and wrists, as the angel's identity reveals herself to me. She is Viviette.

The angel is
Exquisite —
but, somehow,
Familiar.

Madame let me keep this sketch of my 1st full-length gown.
My favorite color— the organza sewn tight 'cross the bosom— so Scandalous!

ORDER OF DANCES.

1. Grand March   *Tobias*
2. Quadrille   *William*
3. Schottische   *William*
4. Two-Step   *Quincy*
5. Waltz   *William*
6. Two-Step   *Edward Flood*
7. Quadrille   *William*

INTERMISSION.

10. Waltz   *William*
11. Quadrille   *Tobias*
12. Quadrille Waltz   *William*
13. Mazurka   *Edward*
14. Waltz   *William*
15. Schottische   *Tobias*
    Quadrille   *Quincy*
    uadrille   *Toby*
ME SWEET HOME.   *Will!*

His majesty cannot be found!

⚜ HARVARD UNIVERSITY. ⚜

.. Dinner and Dance ..

AT THE

Boston Cultural Society, Park Street, Boston

WEDNESDAY, APRIL 18TH, 1863

⟶ MENU ⟵

Consommé Printanier.   Crême Médicis

Saumon, Sauce Mousseline.
Blanchaille.

Petite Caisse à la Royale.

Agneau Rôti, Sauce Menthe.
Haricot Verts Nouveaux.   Pommes au Beurre

Poulet de Printemps Rôti.
Lard Grillé.
Salade.

Asperges en Branches.

Compôte de Fruits au Liqueur.
Gelée Moscovite.

Bombe Glacé.

Dessert.

VERITAS.

9.

Maybe Mister Geist listed it as part of her daily chores!" Mavis snorts with amusement.

"Oh, certainly." I tick off the duties on my fingers. "Lay the grates, polish the andirons, dress up in bedsheets and pose as an angel, dust the bookshelves…"

Mavis presses her knuckles to her mouth so that Aunt Clara won't hear her giggling fits. We are standing outside Aunt's bedroom waiting for Madame Broussard to finish taking orders and measurements.

In days past, after Madame has finished with Aunt Clara she attends to me, and so I am waiting on Mrs. Sullivan's command. "Madame can't leave this house without seeing to you, Miss Jennie. Hard to say if your frocks are more disrespectful to the living or the dead," the housekeeper had clucked.

It's the dismal truth. Both of my mourning dresses are threadbare at the elbow and discolored along the seams. Hardly any of my original buttons—and neither of my original collars—remain. It has been more than two years since I've owned anything new, and my old, black-dyed frocks strain against the predictable directions where I've filled out.

Mavis lingers. Madame Broussard is widely thought to be the handsomest woman in Brookline, and Mavis craves a glimpse of her. "That so-said spiritualist is swindling Mister Pritchett worse than a snake oil salesman," she declares as she stoops to peer through the keyhole.

"I suppose." I won't confide to Mavis the details of my near-fainting spell and how Will had come to me. That entire morning seems unreal, especially in light of Geist's housemaid hoax.

Mavis straightens. "Don't pay him a penny when you go over tomorrow—oh, *bon-jer*, Madame."

For the door has opened and now the striking dressmaker stands before us. Her jet hair is accessorized by tortoiseshell pins, and her dress is the color of claret. In contrast, I feel as shabby as a dormouse.

Mavis is unabashedly delighted by Madame, and for a moment, I, too, feel a shy desire to dip a curtsy. And yet it wasn't very long ago that Madame Broussard had presented me with gown sketches for the annual Boston Cultural Society Dance, an event that Will and I had attended to celebrate his entrance to Harvard, and where I'd taken my first sips of champagne and danced my first waltz. How can my very own memories feel as if they don't belong to me? They seem so extravagant and carefree. Who was that pampered girl in French silk who believed in only happy endings?

Madame nods and moves to step past.

"Please, Madame," I falter. "If you're not late for another appointment, I'm in some need…" I pluck at my skirt, which tells the sad story.

Her fine, dark eyes are guarded. "*Mais*, Mademoiselle Lovell, your aunt has made it clear to me that you won't be fitted for anything new this season. When I asked, she gave me the impression that your present wardrobe is more than adequate."

Though one look at my dress refutes this point. It's hard to say who is more pained by the discomfit of the moment. "Yes, now I remember." I hasten to fill the pause. "Excuse me. I'd forgotten that I'm having two dresses made over secondhand from Aunt." I imagine Aunt Clara smirking from her chaise, and my face burns with shame and rage.

"Madame Pritchett has more than enough material to take in," agrees Madame, too quickly. "So that is a fine solution. *Très simple*."

I step back to let her pass.

She lingers a moment. "*Ma chère*," she says. "My heart breaks for your tragedy. Your brother, and then Monsieur William...*il est tout trop tragique*." The press of her hand to my cheek is more comfort than I have received from any of my kin. Her fingers stop to pick up the edge of my collar. "Such very delicate work."

"It's Miss Jennie did it herself," Mavis bursts out. "She's a grand talent with lace. She fashioned me a fancy collar, too, but I only wear it Sundays. I got a knack for mending, but Miss Jennie has such patience for the details."

"Impressive," says Madame, with a sincerity that makes me blush.

I accompany her to her carriage. Outside, Quinn strides along the garden wall. He is bundled into his overcoat and muffler, yet his face isn't so obscured that I cannot see his lips move. Of the two brothers, Quinn had cut a finer figure in society, where his good looks and quick wit served him better than Will's raw enthusiasm and tendency to speak his mind. But without a captive audience, Quinn is a lonely soul, and time has taught me that he never wants company on these garden walks.

The garden paths were Quinn's retreats whenever he and his brother quarreled. Will, outspoken and fiery, never stayed at Pritchett

House, but took his temper elsewhere, either into town or deep into the country, where I might find him skipping stones or rowing across Jamaica Pond, churning up its waters, exhausting himself.

In contrast, Quinn simply froze in place when he was angry. Housebound, he brooded in his room or haunted the grounds like a lost pup.

He is frozen still. Madame's point of vision follows Quinn as he marches along, locked in battles from which his mind can't escape.

"Poor boy," she murmurs. "So the stories are true."

"What do you mean?" I can hear my own voice strain.

Her glance at me is both sympathetic and faintly pitying.

And though I wish she wouldn't, Madame continues to observe him through the window until her carriage rolls away.

1239 Sankaty Light House, Nantucket

HEINRICH GEIST

MEDIUM PHOTOGRAPHER

Tremont Street
Boston, Massachusetts

"Haunting is the
Undertow" —
is Will trying
to drown me?

 **10.**

I 'm late for the next afternoon's appointment. Geist is waiting in the foyer, and he greets me with coltish energy. Viviette, eyes averted, collects my damp cloak. I'm annoyed to see her. If I don't know the difference between one of heaven's own angels and an ordinary housemaid, then how easily might I be fooled again?

"You don't have to be so coy," I tell her. "I recognize your face."

In answer, she stares up at me with eyes hard and dark as coal, and I realize there's nothing shy about Viviette at all.

"Miss Lovell," says Geist. "At last."

"Please excuse my delay," I say. "Ice on the tracks put the trains off schedule."

Geist shrugs. "At least you are here in one piece. This way, please. There is something I want you to see."

"No, I can't stay," I protest. "I only want to pay the balance and to collect the photograph for my uncle."

"A minute, a minute." Geist pinches hold of my forearm, ushering me down the hall and into the same sitting room where we'd gathered two days before. He points to his ornate French mantel clock, its face adorned with sturdy pink and gold cherubs.

"Behold!" His voice trumpets.

I peer closer. "Yes, I see that your clock is wrong. It is stopped at half past twelve, when it must be nearly…three o'clock?"

He harrumphs. "*Thirty-two* minutes past twelve. And—" He pivots me by both shoulders so that I'm staring into the opposite corner, up at the moon phases and dials of his grandfather clock.

"Thirty-two minutes past twelve," I read.

"Precisely."

"I'm not sure how this concerns—"

"—and I hadn't noticed it, either, until you all had left. Think, Miss Lovell! Two days ago, at twelve thirty-two, in this very room, you experienced some sort of emotional chaos. It penetrated you so deeply, in fact, that you fainted."

I turn from the clock. "You're telling me that my fainting spell stopped time?"

"No, no, no." Geist taps his fingertips together, urging my conclusion. "Twelve thirty-two. The very moment when William Pritchett made contact with you, yes?"

I freeze. "Sir, you are playing games with me," I say. "You stopped these clocks yourself."

"What?" He looks puzzled. "But why would I do that?"

"Why, because…because you know I took the Harding photograph. That I recognized your angel, Viviette, and you caught a change in my manner." I rush on as his chicanery becomes clear to me. "Yes, you saw a change in me as soon as I reentered the room. You knew I'd seen the photograph. And now you're scrabbling to make me a believer again."

"A believer?" He looks baffled. "To what end?"

"Many of us have lost loved ones to this war. Photographing their so-called spirits makes for easy business. Your reputation is everything. You need to convince us of your worth so that you can run your shop."

"Ah. I see." Geist pulls at his beard. "That would be clever of me. But you are incorrect, Miss Lovell. I didn't touch either of these clocks. At twelve thirty-two you received an impression of Corporal Pritchett, did you not?"

"I couldn't confirm that time exactly," I tell him. "And Will is always in my thoughts."

"Tell me, how did you experience this…*thought*? In an ice-cold chill? As a bright burst of energy, or perhaps a flash of radiant—"

"Please, stop." But Geist seems so certain, and I am so taken aback by his certainty, that I blurt out the very question that has been chasing itself around my head. "Mr. Geist, just say you might be correct. Why would Will's spirit contact me *in your home*? A setting that was special to neither of us?" My voice is pained. "I've sat for hours in Will's rooms, walked his paths, and paced the bridge we crossed nearly every summer day. He is nowhere. Nowhere but at rest." I draw myself to my full height, which is not very much.

"A spirit cannot choose his domain," says Geist.

"On that I think you're wrong."

His shaggy eyebrows lift. He's listening. I wish my voice were more dependable. "My twin brother, Tobias, alters my perceptions daily. His spirit is folded into mine. He haunts me. *I* am his domain."

I anticipate that Geist, a man who makes his living grasping for spectral signs, will be intrigued by my revelation. But the photographer is dismissive. "Miss Lovell, how did your brother pass?"

"Of dysentery, a few weeks after he'd joined up."

"My sincere condolences." Geist allows a moment. "But don't

you think you absorb Tobias's identity because he is already so beloved by you? It's not that he haunts you. It is that your memory won't let him go. Simple as that."

I shake my head. "But I'm equally unwilling to let go of Will."

"Aha. And that is where I can show you the distinction." Geist rocks back on his heels, adapting a more philosophical tone. "Miss Lovell, have you ever swum in the sea?"

"Yes." I feel my body tense, remembering the smell of brine, the chop and tug of the water, my abject fear of drowning, a sensation that can frighten me even today. "A few summers ago Uncle took us all to Nantucket."

"And you know the difference between the wave and the undertow?"

I nod.

"Then you will understand my metaphor." Geist speaks with care, as if worried that I might miss a word. "For if memory is the wave that buoys our grief, haunting is the undertow that drags us to its troubled source. I don't speak lightly when I tell you that William Pritchett reached for you because he has unfinished business in this world."

"Mr. Geist, how can you be so sure?"

"I've worked as a medium for many years and have learned some, shall we say, tricks of the trade. This was no trick. Corporal William Pritchett was with us that day, in this room, at thirty-two minutes past twelve. The sensation was very strong and very real." The air seems to vibrate with his conviction.

Geist presses his advantage. "Let me photograph you. For I am sure—"

Another photograph. So Geist thinks I'm holding my own purse strings. That I'm a proper Boston heiress, easily parted with my generous allowance. "Mister Geist, really. I must go. And rest assured, the tricks of your livelihood are safe with me. I'm no gossip."

Not quite true, as I have already confessed plenty of Geist's mischief to Mavis, who *is* a gossip. Not that she could tell anyone who'd care.

His lips thin with displeasure, but he leads me to the hall, where he retrieves the brown-wrapped parcel. "These are two albumen prints from the original negative. One is yours. I thought you might want a copy for yourself."

"You are very kind." In my head I am already adding it to my book.

"Take the time to examine it."

I open the packet to examine the cardboard-backed prints, identical but for a slight shift in hue.

Drained of his rosy pink cheeks and blue-green eyes, Uncle Henry appears bald and dull, whereas Aunt Clara's jellied bulk affords her a dignity that eludes her in real life. From the way Quinn stands, one hand on the back of the love seat, he could be my protector.

I stare at my own image and feel as though I hardly know myself. The angel Viviette hovers above us.

"But how did it happen?" It confounds me. "Viviette wasn't in the room."

"Her image is fixed on another negative," Geist explains, sheepish and proud at once. "I have many. Some of aged grandmothers, or babies and children, or young men dressed in the uniforms of soldiers or sailors. I tailor to a wide variety of loss. A sitter can be convinced that the spirit in the photograph is an exact likeness of one who has passed. We spiritualists call that "recognition." None of my

Union boys matched your Will, but I suspected your aunt would respond strongly to an angel. And so I simply exposed Viviette's plate briefly through the printing process so that she would superimpose upon the next photograph."

Scornful as I am of the gimmickry, Geist's aesthetic impresses me.

"We had some luck," Geist comments, staring over my shoulder. "A cloudless day, a perfect diffusion of light." He pauses. "Viviette looks ethereal."

I have to agree. She is radiant.

And yet something's not quite right about the angel maid. I look and look from print to print, but the difference is maddeningly elusive.

My doubts tug at me long after I have paid the balance and left Geist's townhouse to begin the long walk from Scollay Square to South Side Station, where I will purchase a ticket for a second-class bench on a train that won't get me home until dark.

Stevensburg Virginia March the 11th 1864

Dearest Sister,

I hope this letter finds you in Good Health. My Condition of like is good I am doing well as can be Expectd. We are prety settled down in the camp at Stevensburg I am in a tent with our cousins as well as 2 Irish lads come from Boston a strange man I think he is german he dosnt say much atall

Thank you for yr kind letter of 2 weks past. I am truly sory that you feel I hav Abandond you to the clutchs of Aunt Clara but you know ther was no where else we could go could we when Father died you .... in det there was .... if Father ....—11

gathr restles thay dont seem to be more to Bosn the books are

not fear Sister we dont seem to be comin to our Eld onyhow soon to

Howevr thet wer dosnt seem to be more God willing that want be the ca

Baby run wild beare the House God willing

Aunt Clara wild beagne who go be a Governes With .... I do love my Anne Sister

Jennie... Will sey also to Send much LOVE.

Pleas remembr me to our Butternut TREE

A SPY MUST engag ALL SENSES

PLES ExcusE My pooR WRitiN.

A SPY must Embrac The Unexpectd.

A Spy is for most a Codebreakr

Imagine ME playing
cards with Quinn —
I rather fancy him the
JACK — perhaps not of
Hearts, tho.

"THE BLACK SHAMROCK, EST. 1698, BROOKLINE MASS

My Jenn

Love

will

THE Black
SHAMROCK
IRISH

1698

"Gentlemen y
Sit dow
Pay what
Drink wh

OLD SHERBURNE ROAD IN BROOKLINE VILLA

illustrations are made from
photographs taken in the United   that his face looked (CONTI   was so sh

Me

Fleur

11.

With Uncle Henry away, Aunt takes supper in her room. I eat with the servants in the kitchen. The table is full. Uncle has hired on some men to help patch a leak in the roof. Raucous and friendly, they all leave afterward for the village and a few more pints and laughs at The Black Eye.

"Don't you ever wish you were a man?" I ask Mavis later, as I'm having my bath in the scullery with Mavis on lookout. It's our new custom, since it doesn't seem fair to ask Mavis—or any of Mrs. Sullivan's overworked day girls—to haul the washtub plus endless buckets of boiled water up the three floors. Besides, the scullery is almost cozy, near as it is to the overheated kitchen.

"Not the fighting part, but for the fun of it," Mavis answers. "Mostly I'd like to roam free and never have to scour pots or have babies or wonder where my husband's catting off to nights. Now, get scrubbing, Miss. Though by the look of your neck 'n' nails, by the time I go in the water'll be gray."

On my way to bed, I check in on Quinn dozing in his armchair by the fire, and I accept his unprecedented invitation to join him for a hand of euchre. The game leaves him animated.

"Let's play another round. For stakes," he says as his fingers expertly shuffle the deck.

"If I had any."

"Poor Fleur!" He smiles.

I smile to hear my old nickname, bestowed by my cousins from my long-ago summertime habit of arranging wildflowers in my hair. Funny, the things Quinn remembers. Of course his mind is as sharp as a nail even now. I curl myself more comfortably in my chair as he deals the deck.

"You seem more at ease these days."

"Perhaps because I have more to see," he says, referring to the fact that against the doctor's orders, he has removed his eye patch. Quinn has a notion that his skin must be exposed to air to heal. I don't tell him how I wish he'd kept it covered, how unnerved I am by his damaged eye that moves back and forth like a trapped fly behind his puffed, blue skin.

"Or perhaps I'm only grateful that after a month home," I continue carefully, "you are paying me any attention at all."

"Not fair, Fleur. We've always been close."

I shrug. *Close* is not a word I'd have used. Though I suppose he has been closer to me than to anyone else since his return. Before the war Quinn was endlessly pursued by the smart young Brookline and Boston set, but he's been home for weeks, and has refused to see any friends. Partly I'm sure it's got to do with his injury, which makes him self-conscious.

"Let me lend you some money for cards," he suggests, a smile playing on his lips, "and you can pay me back later."

"Ha! You have a more optimistic view of my fortunes than I."

Quinn laughs outright, which catches at my heart, he sounds so much like Will. He enjoys cards, and I play longer than I want until the clock in the hall strikes twelve long chords. As I leave, I give Quinn's unshaven cheek a quick peck and abscond with the jack of hearts. It's my first kiss for anyone since Will left, and I'm surprised by the spark of feeling it ignites—though of what specific emotion, I'm not sure I could say. My lips feel as if they've brushed fire, and my heart trips in my ribs. Does Quinn notice? I avert my head as I hasten to the door.

"Jennie." At my name I stop. "A question."

I pause and turn.

"Did you really love my brother?" Quinn asks. "Or did you just love him back?"

I can't hide that I'm startled. "What do you mean?"

Casually, he says, "The oldest son. The heir of Pritchett House. You would have been put in a sticky position if you'd rejected his advances. You know how…persuasive Will could get."

"I wasn't *forced* to love Will." A nervous laugh catches and dies in my throat.

"No. Not overtly." Quinn looks uncomfortable. "Ah, I'm being an ass. When all I wanted to comment on was your sweetness, Jennie. You give so freely of your time and good humor, I wondered if Will and I ever realized how much we depended on it."

Then he selects a book from a stack on the carpet and opens it, pretending to be absorbed, and clearly embarrassed by his confession.

Quinn's newfound sensitivity is touching. I'm happy that he has spoken his brother's name, even if the question he posed was odd. I had never conceived of rejecting Will, but I assumed it was because I loved him, not because I feared any consequence. But the hour has grown late for such prickly introspections.

Though I'd set a fire before dinner, it has died and the room is cold. The glass is frosted over, and my candle is a single star in a dark sky. I pull out my scrapbook and page through notes from Toby, uneven and misspelled; letters from Will, with his elegant script and stilted declarations of love; still more scraps of paper, oddities, and curios, before I reach the pages I have kept from Will's sketchbook. Where I find him again. His best gift was for capturing the outdoors. A thread of black ink becomes a bird wing or loop of ivy. I linger over them before turning to a section in the back with drawings, some of myself, where I compare Will's art with Geist's print.

Will's pen unlocks my secret moments. My smile on the cusp of laughter. The breeze in my unbound hair. The bow of my neck against the sun. *Fleur*. I'd forgotten. It's a name that conjures summers past when I gathered starflowers, bluebonnets, thistle, and daisies on the riverbanks, twining them into bracelets and crowns, filling vase after vase, setting them on every windowsill and mantel, much to Aunt's dismay.

But in Geist's print I glower. As if my closed mouth might hide a pair of fangs. We are all dour, all but Viviette, who looks positively beatific.

And then I see what has eluded me. This fragment of detail is now so clear, and yet so radically different, that for a moment I wonder if I've lost my mind.

Quickly, I pry the paper from its backing and bring the candle close. And yet I'm sure my memory is serving me correctly and that the discrepancy is real. Unlike the Harding photograph or the print that I'd set on Uncle Henry's desk, in this image Viviette's head is crowned not by holly berries but by a wreath of dark flowers.

But. The negative could not have changed.

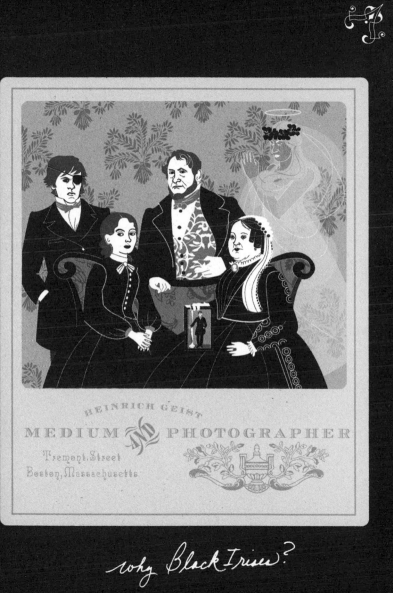

HEINRICH GEIST

MEDIUM AND PHOTOGRAPHER

Tremont Street
Boston, Massachusetts

why Black Irises?

Irises. I trace them with my fingertip. They are inky flames leaping around the angel's head. Transfixed, I can feel myself slipping away again. Geist had called it the undertow, and that strange word now redefines itself as I skid deep into memory.

An August day, the angry sun. Wildflowers and smeared black ink on the sketchbook pages.

My eyes snap open. Black irises. Is there such a flower?

The ink is so dark. Geist's words sliver through my heart. *William Pritchett reached for you because he has unfinished business in this world.*

In the print my own black eyes stare up at me, reproachful. Black pupils, black irises. What am I looking at that I can't see?

A spy must engage all senses.

Taste, touch, smell, sight, hearing. But I can't smell or touch or taste these flowers. "Why black irises?" I murmur aloud. What is the significance of this flower in particular? And in the next breath, I think I might know.

They represent two of the unfortunate prisoners as they appeared upon their return from the Richmond prisons. Dr. ELLERSLIE WALLACE, in sending the photographs, writes as follows :

These two pictures are what may be called good specimens of the bad cases which are brought to the hospital from the prisons and Belle Isle. They are from the worst of the cases, and these worst cases form a numerous body. Both are dead.

Out of one hundred bad cases brought in by boat on May 2 thirty have since died. Dr. VANDERIEFT said they " died from the effects of neglect and c e treatment a, the hands of e, enemy." Dr. V. is an honora e upright, and warm-hearted ge e man. The question is asked, "I se condition of the originals of t n, pictures entirely due to starva h or is there not some disease wh is has reduced them?" I answer of by giving the statements of tw a the men, which are, with on ce, little variation of time and pl of the statements of very many d. all, in fact, whom I questio d The various ones whom I of question were in different par in the hospital, had been brough ve at different times, and could er had no collusion with each o in answering my questions.

I take from my note-book firs M. statement of Corporal W ny SMITH, aged 22 years, Com ky D, Eighth Regiment Kent Infantry :

"I was captured in Septer er, 1863 ; was on Belle Isle six ys and nights without shelter. ey took away my blanket and g I cloth. It rained two or three d nd lay at night in the cold dev ng frost. While in prison, after le ot Belle Isle, in December, he small-pox. I wore the as summer clothes in which er captured ; I lay on the floor; I ny had any thing to sleep on he After I got well my had to was all om th tal

CES ent o derati continuo n the precedin ations which afford relief proof on point. These illustrations are made from is This p photographs taken in the United hief that his face

"THE BLACK IRIS TAVERN, KEPT BY MR. ROGER MOREHEAD ES'D 1698."

My Jennie
Love
Will

THE Black IRIS
1698

"Gentlemen you are Welcome Sit down at yr EASE Pay what you Call for & Drink what you Please."

SHERBURNE ROAD IN BROOKLINE VILLAGE

A Spy advances on Evry Opportunity

12.

Mavis would hate to hear that she snores worse than Mrs. Sullivan. Her sound sleep is my good luck as I fumble for my clothing, rank with soot and sweat from my trip to the city.

My movements are deft and noiseless. For what I need to do, I can't risk Mavis discovering that I've been out. The use of a fresh frock would betray me.

It's just a guess, less than a hunch, but the lights have lit my mind. I won't be able to sleep or to think of anything else unless I am proved right or wrong. I move like mist down the stairs and beeline to Uncle Henry's study.

He has put the photograph in his Indian cabinet and has removed his magnifying lens from its case. In its proximity to the photograph, I gather he might have been using the lens to comb the image for deeper insights.

In Uncle's photograph, Viviette wears her crown of holly.

Just as I'd suspected, it is only my print that has been altered. Its encrypted irises are for my eyes only. I close the door to his study and am off.

The Black Eye, as I'd always heard the tavern called, stands on the outskirts of Brookline Village, at the far end of Sherburne Road near Heath Street. Hurrying alone this late at night on the stretch of road that leads into the village, I am struck by a thousand terrified imaginings. I don't trust my eyes. A hungry beast crouches, ready to rip my flesh from bone. Wild creatures spy from tangled boughs above while a crone crouches behind a tree, beckoning, her gaunt arm a ragged branch. I try to keep my senses sharp. But when a fox darts across my path, I scream and start running. My borrowed boots drag and squelch, but I don't stop sprinting until I have cut across Heath Street, where I spy what must be the tavern.

It's a modest, two-story building, but its swinging lantern is strong enough to be a beacon to its hitching posts, where a few weary horses stand in wait.

And then I see the sign. I am exhilarated and terrified.

One woodcut flower blooms below the elegant letters that spell out the tavern's name. I read it over and over. Until tonight, I have misheard the shorthand slang for it.

The Black Eye, the Black I, The Black Iris. In my hand is the newspaper that I'd stolen from the hired man's satchel, with its back-page advertisement that I'd seen printed a hundred times before. Not a black eye, but a flower.

I push through the door into a room wreathed in smoke from the brick hearth that blazes at the far end. A teakwood bar, twice as large but half as nice as Uncle Henry's, is captained by a pip of a man who stands behind it.

"Good evening," I muster.

"Who you here for?" A dog with a bite.

In addition to Mrs. Sullivan's rubber boots, I'd borrowed Mavis's cloak and bonnet. I'd hoped that entering The Black Iris disguised as a servant would be less conspicuous than a young lady in heeled boots and a trimmed hat.

Dressed as a servant, unfortunately, also means being treated as one.

"Oh...I..." I take quick peeks all around. *A spy must absorb everything and reveal nothing.*

It's men here, mostly. I recognize the roofers seated at the far corner, and I'm thankful to be faced with their backsides instead of their scrutiny. At the wall, younger fellows play darts. Around a more raucous table, mixed sexes cluster. The only face I know is Peg O'Leary's, who Aunt Clara engages twice a year to help with changing over the household linen. Tonight, with her plumped cleavage on show, Peg is more temptress than laundress.

It's a welcome space against the chapping cold, but doesn't feel entirely friendly. Nor does the barkeep's face, with his mouth now down-bent like a brook trout's.

"I'm...I'm..." How to explain myself?

His own conclusions startle me. "I know who you are. You're his Frances. We'd begun to think you'd given him the slip. But you came 'round, after all. He's been waiting for you, then."

Confused as I am, I decide to nod knowledgeably.

The barkeep jabs his thumb toward a walled set of stairs behind him. "Well, get on up. Sue's not here, if you're wondering. Not at this hour. Got her own home and family when she's not tending orphans. Takes after her mother that way. Up the stairs and turn the corner. You'd be his first visitor in two weeks."

"Thank you, sir." It seems safe, for now, to pretend to be Frances.

"Sir's my father. Now, scat. He's waiting."

My mind is manic as I go. Have I been directed here through

some otherworldly connection to find Will? Has he been injured, traumatized to a point where he has possibly mistaken me for a young woman named Frances?

Yes, yes, yes. It all makes perfect sense. Will is here, right here at the Black Iris, and he's been here all along, waiting for me.

I am so ready to believe in something good as I hurry up the steps and around the corner to yank open the closed door that I'm not at all prepared for what lies behind it.

Nate Dearborn —
late of the 28th
Massachusetts Volunteer
Infantry

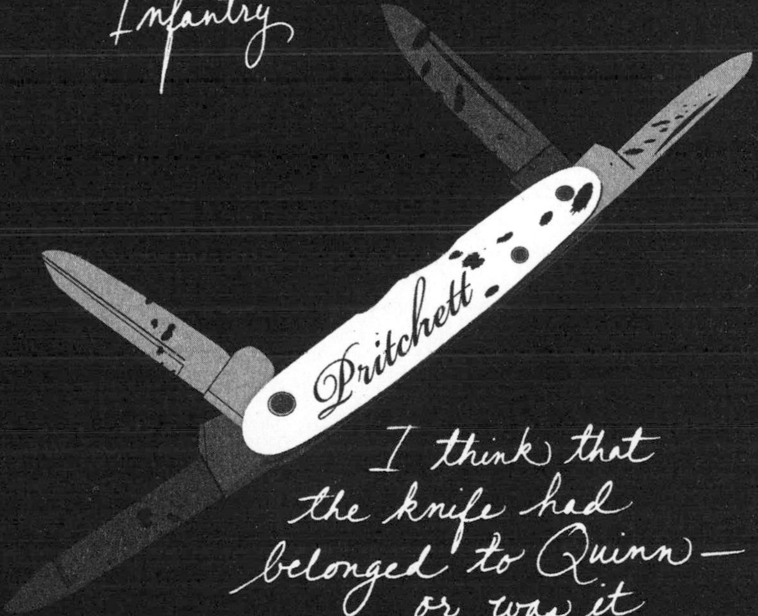

I think that
the knife had
belonged to Quinn —
or was it
Will's ?

13.

He sits in the dark, in a chair pulled up against the night window, smoking. I try not to cough, but fail.

It's not William. Of course not. But I am light-headed nonetheless from the ether of hope as I fix a purposeful smile to my face. "I'm sorry." I squint to see him. "Am I...interrupting you?"

"Sue props me up," he says in a quarrelsome tone, "and then forgets about me. Poor old Sue, I'd wager she's got a lot to remember. Good of her to send you, though."

"She didn't send me. I don't know Sue. And I'm not Frances," I say awkwardly.

"Well, I can see you're not Frances—blindness ain't my problem." He taps his pipe and scowls at me through the shadows. "I'm Private Nathaniel Dearborn. Before that, back in Pittsfield, I was Nate."

"Should I call you Nate?"

"Huh. If you want."

"May I light the candle?"

"If you want."

I've already struck a match. Lit, the bedside candle stub

illuminates the face of this round, freckled boy who is no more than my age, though his gaze is world-weary. "Pittsfield? That's forty miles away."

"I told 'em home was Brookline—it's not as if they check those things. Dump you off, and no questions asked. That's how it's done. Sue found me like a drownded puppy in the hospital, and she gave me some dignity when she brought me here. For which I am grateful. But I need a favor, Miss not-Frances," says Nate in a voice that wishes he didn't. "Will you put me to bed?"

It's an unusual request, but as I move closer I understand. Beneath the blanket piled on his lap, Nate is missing both of his legs.

I set my teeth to hold any disgust from my face. "I can try." As he tamps out his pipe, I place the candle on the sill, drop the hood of my cloak, and tie back its sleeves to free my arms. He is heavy, but once I tug the chair closer to the bed, Nate can do the rest. He hauls up the weight of his body on the sinewy strength of his arms. Then swings himself over and onto the mattress as I hold the chair steady.

Positioned, Nate leans back and groans. "Thought I'd be up at that window all night."

"It sounds as if this Frances should be here tending to you. Is she your sister?"

He looks at me with eyes that are two hostile, scorched marks in his face. "Frances Paddle, that's my girl," he tells me. "She's a ladies' maid to a smart couple down in New York City. It's not your business why she ain't collected me yet."

"I'm sorry." But I press on. "Does she know what happened to you?"

"Doubtful." He exhales. "That's the thing about Fran. She ain't really here. Back when we were crossing South Mountain, I made her up inside my head. I could imagine her face so clear, 'specially when there weren't enough rations and I had to fill up on something. Every night I held her in my dreams. Now I'm so used to her, I can't give her up. She's real as my legs."

I can only nod. Dumbfounded.

"Don't pity me." Nate throws me a scathing look. "You don't know how you'd want to spend your days and nights if it'd happened to you. Who are you, anyhow, if Sue din't send you? Why're you here?"

"My name is Jennie Lovell. And I'm not sure why I've come, except—"

But Nate's expression has changed so completely that I stop.

"Jennie Pritchett?" His freckles seem to stand out in his pale face. A reverse constellation.

"Oh, yes. Yes!" I am alert at once. "I mean, no. Pritchett's my uncle."

"Aw, it's impossible. You think I'm a fool?" Nate waves me off. "Look at you, you ain't his cousin. You're not but a servant girl. My boy Pritchett wouldn't've got hitched to some chit. Got to wake up earlier to put me on."

By now I've yanked off Mavis's bonnet and am pulling at the pins that hold up my hastily dressed hair. My proof is irrefutable, I know—Will loved my curls and would have described them to anyone, if he'd ever spoken of me.

As my hair tumbles loose, Nate allows himself a glance. And then a slow, sly smile. "He said you had hair like a storm. Not the beauty I pitchered, but all right, so be it...you must be Pritchett's Jennie. Reckon you've come down in the world in your servant's clothes, eh?" And quick as a mousetrap, his fingers swipe for a lock of my hair, which he pulls hard and then releases with a bullying laugh that hints at the young man he once was.

Automatically, I back out of his range, though the young soldier seems hungry for contact. And I do pity him. How couldn't I? To be alone for hours in this room, prisoner of a wrecked body, would be a hell on earth.

Nate knows he has scared me. He softens. "You being here, however you found me, and him *not* here." He clears his throat. "That means he's dead, then, huh?"

I can hardly bear to confirm it. "Yes."

He reaches for his pipe and relights it. Accepting this fresh grievance blank-faced, though I sense the news wounds him into silence. I wait.

"'Fore I planned my escape," Nate says, finally, "he gave me a letter. Says if I got out alive, I was to get it to you."

My heart thrums. "A letter."

"Yup. And as you can see, I got out, only to get shot down not two days later, mistook for a Grayback—so they said. Shattered both my legs. I was left without hope. When the Union boys found me, they sawed 'em off at once with hardly enough chloroform to take me out. But I held on to that letter. I din't go back on my word. Blast it, I even paid a fellow to find you. The crook cabbaged my dime and told me nobody lived there by the name Jennie Pritchett. I know firsthand how a fellow can invent a girl from scratch and make her come alive. So then I guessed that you were a hoax, too. Same as Fran. Made me laugh. Pritchett spoke of you so convincing."

"I don't understand. It'd be easy to find Pritchett House. Everyone knows it."

"Huh, it was that that stuck-up brother sent him away, and without any explanation. For *he* found his way home, din't he? Snot-nosed bastard; he was sweet on you, too. Brother against brother. A damn disloyalty, if y'ask me." Nate's sudden burst of anger is unnerving—it's apparent that he's no friend to Quinn. "Top drawer. I know it's itching ya." He points to the battered dresser, thick with paint, wedged in the corner.

In that smile of his I see another flash of this more brutal and dangerous Nate. Sweat breaks out on my forehead.

"Thank you for trying to find me," I manage to say. "I owe you a favor, and I can start by helping you right now if you want to get home to Pittsfield. I've got a bit of savings, some jewelry that I could sell—" Aunt Clara's brooch, for one. Brazenly pinned to a page of my book.

His hand severs the air. "Like I said, I'm never going back. Not in this life. War was my best way out, and I intend to stay out. I slipped that noose once; that's better'n others fared. As for Sumter, welp, call it our nature or our destiny. We picked the adventure knowing there'd be no end but a bloody one. Got more good luck than I deserved when Sue took pity. An eyeful of your curls is the sugar icing on my cake." Again, Nate grasps for my hair, fingers quick as a monkey, but I am quicker as I dart to the bureau.

My hand roves among his few shabby items—his identification papers and long underwear and folded neckerchiefs, a print of himself in his uniform, all brash and swagger, and a penknife that I'm quite sure belonged to Uncle Henry, before it was acquired by one of his sons. I slip both the photograph and knife into my cloak pocket with a twinge of guilt, for poor Nate has so few worldly treasures. My fingers spider around in the dark drawer for any other missed particulars, and I pull out an onionskin envelope, marked only with the letter *J*.

It is as if Will couldn't quite commit to addressing it. Seeing it, however, I know what it means to feel one's blood freeze.

With everything tucked safely in my possession, I turn. "Thank you for this."

Nate looks uneasy. "You won't tell Sue? Or ole Wigs—for he'd chuck me out of his pub in a heartbeat and leave me for wolves if he learnt it."

"I won't tell…" Though I don't understand what I am promising.

"'Twas a different world, Sumter was. You'd have to live through it."

My fingers rub the crinkled paper. "What—where is Sumter?"

"Camp Sumter; it's in Georgia. It's where we got sent after they took us," Nate explains, impatient when I still don't understand. "The Succesh prison, of course. You must have known that much."

"Oh…yes." My hand crushes the envelope tighter. Will's last letter has confused me. He was killed in battle, not captured.

"They've been good to me here, Sue and her ole Wigs. And I'm not here for long. For it's crawling up on me, see—" Nate swipes back the blankets and begins undoing the binding around what's left of one of his legs.

"Please, don't—"

But he won't stop, and what he reveals to me is the stuff of nightmares, far worse than Quinn's bludgeoned eye.

The flesh of Nate's legs is rotten. Even by flickering candle-light I see that his skin, mottled and sticky with pus, is also rancid with infection.

It is revolting, and horrifying, and almost too sad to bear. I cup a hand to my nose and mouth to stop myself from gagging. "Where is the doctor to tend to this? No matter, I will send ours."

"They brought one, Norris. He's a dentist, so he should know when parts are rotted. He said it's rotted too deep, but that weren't news to me." And yet the sight of his own leg seems to have panicked Nate. He hides his knees with the blanket, his fingers spreading and smoothing the fabric as if to erase the vision. "Stay a spell, Fran. Tell me about the good days. How it used to be between us. Please, dear? I want a pretty memory in my head."

Shaking my head, I back away from him, toward the door. "I'll come and visit again, just as soon as I can, with our own doctor. And I'll bring you some books, too. They'd be good company for you."

"Don't want 'em. Can't read 'em. Fran, stay awhile. Smoke a pipe with me. I've got a whole raft of Durham tobacco under my mattress. Please, Fran?"

No, no, no. I shake my head, I can't bear to hear anymore. Tomorrow I'll send someone with a crock of soup and blankets, and a note for Doctor Perkins. But I can't stay here a moment longer.

Nate continues to entreat me. "Please, Frances, darling? Won't you please?"

"I'm so sorry...so sorry." Head tucked, I hurry from the room and close the door. Nate's voice follows me down the stairs and echoes in my ears, even after I've escaped the tavern, and Wigs's gimlet stare, and have headed back out into the night.

Dearest Jennie,

I write on this Floor of packed Earth, with little Light
my Hands scratched by Brambles and Blood beneath m[y]
and soaking through my Bandages. Oftentimes these Days
if I chanced to see you on the Street, would you even recognize me? For
I hardly know my Own Reflection. Once I stuck a Man with my
Bayonet so that his Blood splattered hot over my Face. He looked me
square in the Eyes as he fell, and I did not flinch ~~and~~
~~when~~ this was my True Self—

These Weeks since
to be taken Prisoner, which may indeed be
                       though we may never again meet on Earth,
I do want   you to know that I always meant
      not find Trouble, there are many of us in Harm's Way
one broken Neck they say will be an example to others
                         and I know not how to make this Confession
       but to write the Truth of my Love
                    with Hope that you might think of me a little, ~~J~~
                                                                      Jennie

For I am always thinking of you

SUCCESSION

UNION

J.M. WHITTEMORE & CO. 55 WASHINGTON ST. BOSTON

14.

Coming home I'm nearly found out. Luckily the noise is thunderous, and I scamper behind a tree as the carriage clatters past and turns up into our drive.

Uncle Henry, who had been away on business in Scarsdale, must have decided not to stay the night. Now everyone will be waked, and my absence surely will be discovered.

As I approach the house, I see the hired man in his work clothes. I know he'd returned from the tavern only moments before—I'd heard his whistle up ahead of me on the road, and I'd walked well behind him, out of sight. I creep up along the edge of the lawn, darting from tree to tree. One of the boys is unstrapping Uncle Henry's valise from the back, and Mrs. Sullivan is stationed at the door, quiet as a post. Her folded hands waiting to see if Uncle wants her to cook him a late supper before he goes to bed.

Such unrelenting drudgery, the lives of the servants.

Aunt Clara is nowhere in sight. For this, I breathe a calming sigh as I slip around the side of the house in order to enter through the back. If Aunt were awake she'd expect everyone to rouse and tend to her. Which would have made it quite impossible for me to sneak into the house and then pretend I'd been here all night.

Through the pantry, silent at the boot jack, I steal in stockinged feet up the back stairs, where I overhear Uncle Henry in the foyer requesting a sausage pie and brandy in the library. But I am battened down safe in my attic room before he has taken the second flight of stairs.

At last. My heart is knocking in my chest. I build up the fire from its embers and unfold Will's letter, which I read on my hands and knees by the scant heat.

Even before I begin, I can see that it's been written under hardship and duress. Will's letters tremble and slant backward confusedly. What's more, the paper is water damaged, the last passages a wash of ink.

When I am finished, I close my eyes, which burn with the effort of reading this final, agonized missive from the grave. Wherever Will's body is buried, too much of my heart is there, too.

"It doesn't matter, William," I whisper. "None of it matters anymore. For I will always love you, no matter what this war forced you to become. Always and ever, dear heart."

For what else could I say? What else could I ever possibly say about a senseless death and a war that I do not understand?

Stavensburg, Virginia
April the 10th 1864

My Jennie, my Dear One,

I know that I have written you
this before, but I must repeat — how my
heart is breaking for you, and for all of us
— for Tobias' Death has brought Melancholy
over the entire camp, these past weeks.
That he was your twin and Only brother means
that you, more than any of us, know that
not a more lively & gentle Soul ever
existed. I do feel the loss of our Toby
nearly every minute.

If you can possibly summon the strength again
in midst of your grief, I beg you write me, my
dearest Cousin. You have been foremost in my
thoughts these long days in winter camp.
I keep reading and rereading your sweetest letter
of one month past where you said you do
Love Me after all & it brings me such Joy
in this sad place I cannot tell you how much.

I shall describe my circumstances — and perchance
my great Scribbling might distract you from your sorrowful
mind. Well here I am sitting on a hard Oaken
with a sore Rump, for a desk, writing of Yet
between Drillin & Meals & Waiting. Yet
it is not so bad as the Newspapers might
have you believe, those fellows in camp
who remain in Health are quite jolly sorts, though
they are Miles away from being Gentlemen.
I have made the acquaintance of one Charlie,
and he plays cards like the Devil himself
& has a wit to match. Do not roll those eyes
at me, Dear Jennie, how else is a young
restless Soldier to spend his time?

Miss Jennie Lowell
Pritcett House
Brookline, MA

Dearest Jennie,

I write on this Floor of packed Earth, with little Light to see by, my Hands scratched by Brambles and Blood beneath my Fingernails and soaking through my Bandages. Oftentimes these Days I wonder if I chanced to see you on the Street, would you even recognize me? For I hardly know my Own Reflection. Once I stuck a Man with my Bayonet so that his Blood splattered hot over my Face. He looked me square in the Eyes as he fell, and I did not flinch, ~~and I~~ ~~may seldom~~ this was my True Self.

These Weeks since ~~to be taken Prisoner~~, which may indeed be

though we may never again meet on Earth,

I do want   you to know that I always meant
             not find Trouble, there are many of us in Harm's way
one broken Neck they say will be an example to others
~~I~~   and I know not how to make this Confession
          but to write the Truth of my Love
          ~~with~~ Hope that you might think of us a little,   Yours

          For I am always thinking of you

I can barely
recognize his handwriting.
Can he have changed so very much?

114 WASHINGTON ST., BOSTON
SUCESSION

15.

My dreams are bursts and jolts. I see the bloody steel blade of a bayonet. I hear the drum beat to the sound of soldier's boots and feel cold earth, cold hands, a chain, choking me.

I awake into a glare of morning and the sound of a voice.

"Saints above, Miss, what's done you in—drink a bottle of your uncle's spirits last night?"

I sit up, wheezing for breath, my fingers stroking my neck, reassuring myself that it's not broken as my bleary eyes find Mavis staring down on me.

"You think I'm drunk?" I ask faintly, as the horrible dream ebbs away.

Her grin is teasing. "How else could you sleep through breakfast—and all this arguing?"

Sunshine streams through my window. It's rare for me to oversleep, particularly now, on this lumpy horsehair mattress. "Arguing about what?" But I hear it. My bedroom door is ajar, and the voices below are angry. Quinn and Aunt Clara. When I stand, my sore muscles resist. "What about?" I repeat.

"Everything!" Mavis enthuses. "It's been more delicious than toffee cake. Oh, has Mister Quinn been giving her an earful. It started as something to do with the dressmaker's bill. Old Mister Pritchett will never raise his voice about Missus Pritchett's wastefulness, but it seems Mister Quinn's taken her to task."

I can't resist. I clamber to the banister, the better to hear the voices pitching back and forth below. Quinn's tenor is clear and flat, barely raised at all. "...drowning in costs...well over our annual... damn fripperies...*and* pay for the household expenditures!"

And while Aunt squeaks like a mouse defending her cheese, her words are mysterious. "If you would only assert yourself...you are paralyzed...to make a decision one way or another..."

A decision about what? But next comes the slamming of doors, another of Aunt's childish gestures, and now their conversation is muted.

Mavis clears her throat. "Speaking of household particulars— and it's awkward to ask of you, Miss Jennie—but Missus Sullivan sent me up to see if you'll lend an extra pair of hands. It's brass and silver day. She says t'would only be 'bout an hour or two."

"Of course." Closer to four or five hours, but I don't mention this.

"It's another reason Mister Quinn's upset." Mavis's eyes glint with gossip. "There isn't enough in the ledger to hire more than one day girl. Missus Sullivan spoke with your uncle last night. He said hired girls had been pre-considered in the annual household budget—and what a donkey laugh *that* was. There isn't been a household budget in months, anyway. Missus Pritchett spent the whole lot on clothes and gimcracks like fancy sun parasols and watering cans from London, England."

Mavis can't disguise her annoyance. I sense that Uncle Henry's fumbling inattention has been a topic of servants' talk before. "Quinn mentioned you, too, Miss. He says you're in need of new boots."

I color, surprised that Quinn would have noticed. It lifts my heart that he did.

"And he said you've got no position here," Mavis adds, more quietly. "He didn't say it unkind, Jennie. But he said it."

My heart skips a beat. "He means well by me. He'll set things right," I say, though new doubts shake awake in my head. Does Quinn want me gone? With a new pair of boots for the journey out?

Mavis still looks shy. "Missus Sullivan's holding your breakfast. You better claim it before she gives it to Lotty."

I nod. My mind is a whirl. It will be impossible to get to Geist today. It had been all I wanted to do after last night's revelations—the arrow marked in a wreath of irises that had led me to Will's scrap of letter.

Before I dash to rescue my meal, I open my scrapbook again and rub my fingers against the stained paper. The ink is blotted, the handwriting looks weak. I can almost feel the ache and fatigue in his words, so different from the determined cheerfulness of his other letters.

In bold daylight I am better able to register that Will's last letter is in fact a confession. He had killed. He had stolen. He wrote of suffering and injuries. His last days were not as I'd imagined, cut down in the heat of battle. He died a prisoner. His story is a cry of shame.

Nate carries part of this secret. And so, I am sure, does Quinn.

Something is not right here. I must make sense of the confusion. What sort of raging monster had Will become in the end? What does Quinn intend to protect in his silences and lies? I yank so hard at my bootlaces that my feet feel the pinch as I hasten down the back stairs to the kitchen.

For of course Quinn is protecting his brother. Will's end must have been so wretched that Quinn had to *pretend* he fell in battle. Quinn didn't see his brother die—otherwise Will surely would've given him my locket. I'm speculating, but I'm on the trail of the truth. And I want all of it.

Yet today I'm tasked with servant's chores. There's nothing I can do until they're done. Under Mrs. Sullivan's regime, the polishing of the brass and silver is a tedious matter, set in motion when every item is carried into the dining room and placed on the table. Each object is checked against her ledger before bowl, candlestick, or piece of tea service is transported down to the kitchen, where, the day girl, Lotty, is given the lowest job of all: tarnish scrubber.

The scrubbed silver is then rinsed and re-rinsed, polished and buffed, carried upstairs, and set back upon the table for Mrs. Sullivan to inspect before it's all replaced, safe and sparkling, in its designated position on whatever dreary sideboard, table, or corner cupboard. No amount of sparkle could lighten the gloom that lies over Pritchett House.

We work steady as carpenter ants, the mood of the morning's fight lingering like an acrid burning after the fire's stamped out. Aunt Clara has slunk off to her rooms, and Quinn has locked himself in his. I catch nobody's eye for fear I might blurt out the whole incredible business of the last twelve hours.

Later in the afternoon, as I am replacing the bone-handled carving knives in their chest and Mrs. Sullivan has moved on to dinner preparations, I hear her call for the hired man to kill a chicken for supper.

"He's up on the roof. I'll do it." Quinn's voice. He has left his room, likely creeping down for a cup of bouillon that Mrs. Sullivan, a great believer in the healing powers of bouillon, keeps in a spare kettle on the hearth.

I hear the clatter of cups. "No, no, Mister Quinn, let me pour—"

"It's no trouble. I did quite a bit of hostess duty for the corps." I recognize the old coaxing charm in Quinn's voice that these days he reserves for the servants. It always works. Sure enough, Mrs. Sullivan giggles.

I hear Quinn pass through the kitchen door. I pull on my cloak and hide my tarnished palms in a pair of mittens before I join him in step as he heads out to the yard.

"The almanac promises an early spring," I begin amiably, but Quinn's in no temper to chat.

"Jennie, you should leave here," he says. "Put us out of your life, one and all."

"Where would I go?" I feel a sting my eyes. I think of Nate, trapped at his window.

"There are opportunities." Gracefully, Quinn swoops underhand to catch a speckled guinea, thrusting it into my arms in a single motion. A lock of his hair falls forward, and I resist the impulse to smooth it back into place. We head for the tree stump. *La guillotine*, Toby had called it. "You're very clever."

I can't remember if Quinn has ever outright complimented me before. In light of that kiss, and Nate Dearborn's words—*he's sweet on you, too*—I wonder if he continues to harbor feelings, or if he ever truly did.

"Clever at what?"

His expression is neutral. "You've got a calming way. You could be a nurse, or a governess, even."

"I'm sorely uneducated." I stroke the guinea beneath its gullet to subdue it. Other chickens, sensing danger, are clucking and scuttling around us, clawing up the cold earth. "You know I quit Putterham when Papa died. Besides, I never took to it, not really. I could tell you everything about Prometheus and Epimetheus, thanks to Papa. But I can't multiply higher than ten times ten." I feel the bird go heavy in my arms.

Quinn shrugs. "A pity. I wish I'd got to know your father. History will remember him with respect, as one of the first men to enlist in this war."

"And to get killed in it." Four years ago. It seems another lifetime since the beginning of the fighting. "Toby always said it was suicide. That Papa was never right in his head after our mother passed."

"He wouldn't be the first to go mad with grief. Some days I think I am mad, with what I've seen." Quinn shakes his head as if to displace his thoughts. "The new reports say that the South is bankrupt, and I know firsthand that most of it's destroyed, with a Union victory all but guaranteed. However it ends, I fear it'll be many years we'll be wiping up the blood of our memories."

"Your experiences have left you bitter, Quinn. I'm sure we'll be happy again. That's what Will and Toby would have wanted."

But Quinn doesn't answer. He disappears into the henhouse, and when he returns he has knotted on the blood-rusted butcher's apron and is carrying the axe. He pulls the limp bird from my arms, positions it on the stump, and then—with one sure hand and a single stroke—he severs its neck.

There's a chorus of squawking as the headless chicken begins a jerking death-dance around the yard. Other livestock scatter.

"You used your left hand," I note.

"I favored it as a child," he says, opening his fingers, then closing them into a fist. "Then I was retrained properly at school. Wasn't until I needed to shoot a gun that I went cack-handed again. Now I use my left for everything. It seems to have retained an intuitive skill." He wipes the blood of the blade on his apron before wedging it into the stump. "S'pose I needed any natural advantage for survival."

Doubtless there will never be an easy time to confront Quinn, but the question has been so long on the tip of my tongue, it almost has a taste. I plunge ahead. "Will you tell me what Will met up against before he was killed? I want to know it. He was in trouble, wasn't he?"

"Trouble? He was a hero." Quinn raises his eye patch for a moment and wipes his forehead with the sleeve of his coat. The eye, though less raw, is thickly ridged with scar tissue. Queasy, I look away. "Don't we have a telegram from Captain Fleming? Don't we have a respectable service planned for Will come spring?"

"I deserve better from you, Quinn," I say. "The truth, for example. I know there's more to this story." I don't dare risk telling him about Nate and the letter. Not now.

A spy's sixth sense is timing.

In the barbed silence, we stare at each other, faced with the unassailable wall built of what Quinn refuses to confess.

"And after that service," he says, his voice level, "it might be best for you to leave this house. As I mentioned, there is nothing for you here."

"Except you," I murmur, glancing down at my blood-spattered boots.

"Don't say that, Jennie," His voice breaks. "Not when you don't mean it."

"I'm sorry." Didn't I mean it? I'm confused myself and unable to tear my gaze from his.

By now Mrs. Sullivan has come lumbering across the yard. She scoops the lifeless bird to bleed and pluck, oblivious to what, if anything, has just passed between Quinn and me. "Thank you, Mister Quinn," she says, but he has already turned away.

"Wait! Quinn! I'll walk with you!" I call after him.

His strides are too long for me to keep up. I stop following. Still in his bloodied apron, Quinn crosses under the trellis that leads from the kitchen garden down to the crab apple orchard.

Dismal by winter afternoon, it appears as a trek of starved gray trees and hard-packed soil. Along its path, Quinn moves steady, casting a long shadow that is wafer-thin and lonely as a reaper against the gray sky.

Notice the house keys.

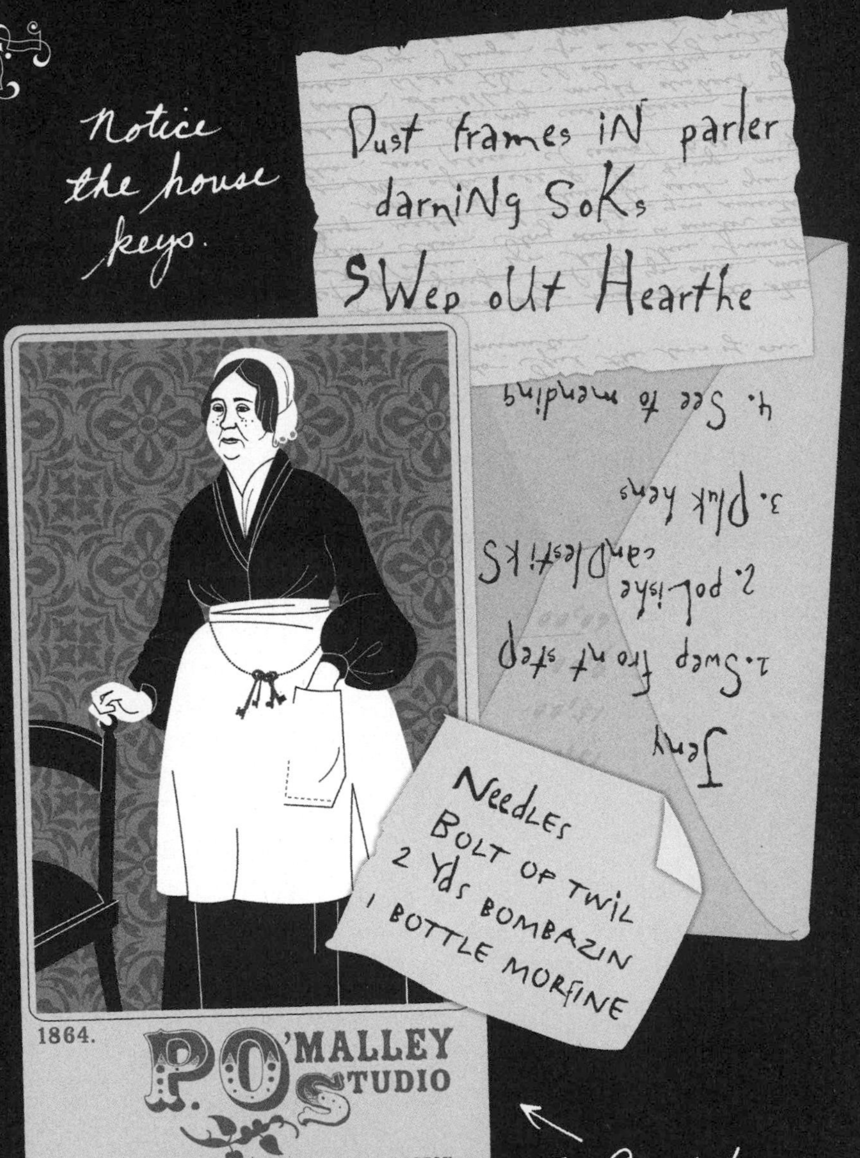

The Cheek!

This bit of Pretension need not reach Mrs. Sullivan's sister.

Boston 16 December 1864

Dry goods purchase order
  for Mrs. Henry Pritchett

2 gal. sugar ———————————— 1.45
5 yds. Irish Linen ———————— 220.00
6 Silver Buttons ———————— 35.00
3 yds. calico ———————————— 75

1 pr. French kid gloves ———— 125.00
2 pkts sewing pins ————————— 10
1 lb. English soap ———————— 1.10
4 pr. cotton stockings ———— 16.00
Beeswax, 1 lb. ————————————— 5.00
5 yds. toweling ———————————— 7.25

by Mr. Wm. H. Kirke

Kirke & Sons, Ltd.

I cannot bear to hand this
over — my poor Uncle Henry.

16.

Although Quinn doesn't bring up my leaving Pritchett House, he has injected the fear into me. Where would I go? What would I do? Over the next few days, I am a mouse in search of a new flowerpot under which to hide.

Homing in on what she (rightly) perceives as my insecurity, Mrs. Sullivan starts to give me lists, misspelled commands on scraps of brown butcher paper, and though she hasn't assigned me the charwoman's work—yet—my hours are spent sweeping, mending, and so much dusting that my lungs ache from sneezes. But I do everything she asks, afraid to raise a fuss.

But by the week's end, when Uncle mentions that he'll be going into town for an early meeting at the bank, I'm resolute. This Saturday is my only chance, for it's when Mrs. Sullivan takes a half day to commiserate with her elder sister, Millicent, over tea in Fort Hill. She flourishes a newly printed *carte de visite* that she'd ordered expressly for the occasion—though it seems a bit of a pretension, considering Millie has been receiving her sister every other Saturday for the past thirty years.

But Mrs. Sullivan has a dozen and surely won't miss one, so

I spirit it into the folds of my apron while she checks her hat in the mirror.

She hurries out, lugging her basket that is no doubt stocked with stolen wares from our pantry. But she doesn't open the carriage door, however, without burdening me with yet another list, this one for items to pick up from Kirke & Sons.

Battleship clouds glower in the sky that morning. I stay downstairs to ensure I'll catch Uncle as he departs. My photograph and letter are hidden in my pocket, and my excuse is writ firm in my head.

"Mrs. Sullivan needs me to go to Merchants Row. Might I ride with you, sir?"

"For dry goods?" Uncle looks befuddled. "Couldn't she send someone else? Next Monday, perhaps?"

"No one can be spared," I demur. "We are sorely understaffed."

His cheeks bloom with embarrassment. "Such are our sacrifices in wartime."

"Yes, Uncle." But he's annoyed. He is a slipshod manager and we both know it.

On the ride into the city, Uncle Henry pays me no mind, though his dossier seems to perplex him. Once, he looks up hard at me, as if trying to calculate my personal worth versus cost, and then it's my turn to blush as I imagine him pondering my financial inconvenience to his family.

And I would go! I want to shout at him. *If I had half an opportunity, I'd leave today!*

"Jennie, I need one word with you about that medium," he remarks as we enter the heart of South Side, lively with Saturday morning hackneys and omnibuses as well as a few street vendors setting up their fruits and flowers.

"Yes?" There's a squeeze in my heart. Does he know my morning's plans?

Uncle brings his pocket watch from his waistcoat and pays excessive attention to polishing its surface. "On further inquiry, it seems this chap Geist is a two-bit fraud. As some of the fellows at the bank explained it, his camera is loaded with mirrors, double images. The specifics are beyond me, but it must not get out that we'd been hoodwinked."

"Our visit was a private family meeting," I jump in to assure him.

"Correct. For there's no reason to doubt William isn't in heaven with the Lord's angels. I don't need proof of it." Uncle blinks rapidly. "S'pose I can see why Geist's business might be a comfort to the uneducated. But we Pritchetts are made of sterner stuff."

"Yes, Uncle. Without doubt."

And that seems to settle it. Still, I worry that Uncle has just sent me a subtle warning against visiting Geist, and so after the carriage lets me off I pay my legitimate call at Kirke & Sons, where I put in an order for needles, rickrack, and a bolt of twill to be charged to our house account, all the while looking over my shoulder to see if Uncle has followed me.

A spy must watch for all options and exits. I can almost hear Toby whisper it, his words a secret spell in my ear.

"We'll deliver by early next week. But your account is three months in arrears," says old Mr. Kirke, looking down over his pince-nez and handing me a sheaf of horrifyingly overdue bills. "You'll need to settle in full."

I nod, mortified, and resolve to hide the bills away as I take leave for Geist's townhouse. How awful. Somebody needs to confer with Uncle Henry about the household debt, but it won't be me. Aunt seems to have lost any ability to manage Pritchett House. Awkward as it might be, perhaps I should speak to Quinn.

Geist opens the door himself, which catches me by surprise. And he has company, which I also didn't expect. His guest resembles my girlish imaginings of Moses. His floss of long white hair is balanced by an equally snowy beard. That, the pouches under his eyes, and his shabby Inverness give him the look of a wandering holy man.

Geist introduces him as Mr. Locke, the war photographer. "He has just returned from a field tour. Thirteen states in six months," says Geist, but Mr. Locke clearly isn't inclined to speak of it. His lips press thinly, and he avoids Geist's eyes as he murmurs in his rasping voice about the promise this year of an early spring and how he will be heading up to Portland come April. The strings and pulleys of his conversation yank our talk far from topics such as where he's come from and what he's witnessed.

Eventually Geist escorts Locke down the steps to a waiting coach.

"Poor man can't even live under the same roof as his most recent work," Geist says as he reenters, bolting the door and rubbing his hands against the cold. "He has given it to me to archive." He gestures to a battered satchel by the stairs.

"May I see?"

"It's nothing you'd want to look at." The photographer grimaces. "Locke has been from Anderson to Shiloh. Most of this winter he followed General Sherman to Savannah, documenting the ruin. He thinks his images will act as living history so that we don't repeat our mistakes." There's no mistaking the skepticism in Geist's tone. Then he rolls back onto his heels, his fingers webbed across his chest. "So what can I do for you, Miss Lovell? For I presume there's a purpose to your call?"

"Yes. You were correct, after all." I give him my print and prepare myself for his astonishment.

He stares, lifts his brows. "Intriguing." He hands it back. "Yet I find it curious that you'd want to dupe me."

"Dupe?" I almost laugh. "You think I meddled with this image?"

"What else should I think?"

Bewildered, I look for what Geist sees. In new light the black curlicues of the iris petals look different. A delicate but all-too-human work of quill and ink. "I swear on my life, sir. I didn't touch it." My finger crosses my heart, a gesture of childlike earnestness—and yet I am feeling increasingly, mortifyingly childlike.

"And I swear on mine, neither did I. And so now we circle each other, wondering who is the charlatan?"

Truly, not the outcome I'd expected. "I don't know what to say…" I falter. "Except that no matter what you think of this photograph, I'm here as a believer. On my last visit, you were convinced that Will's spirit had come to me. I couldn't bring myself to admit it at the time. I'd had a vision right in your parlor, of one afternoon during my last summer with Will, when a prankster had destroyed his sketchbooks by pitching them into the water. But then it was more than a memory. It was as if Will had conjured his very life energy to stand before me."

Geist is listening. I take it as a sign to continue. And so I confess my choking nightmares and my belief that the black irises in the photograph linked me to my discovery of Private Dearborn, which couldn't possibly be pure coincidence.

Finally, I take Will's letter from my purse and hand it to him. Geist opens it and reads.

"You see, it's my proof," I tell him. "Will must have got himself into some terrible trouble, before the end." My fingers twist at the place where my engagement ring once sparkled. I'm as unused to its absence as I was to its weight. "Whatever Will has done, perhaps he wants to communicate something to me. I think he wants me to know that he is angry—enraged—about something. Just like that day by the lake. If your photo—"

"He mentions yellow jackets and mosquitoes," Geist interrupts, lifting his eyes from the letter. "A pestilence of summer."

It takes me a moment to understand. "But hardly ever found in spring," I say slowly. "Will was killed May sixth."

"He was *reported* killed. You saw the telegram?"

I nod, thinking of it in my book. "I did. Signed by a Captain Fleming."

The spiritualist looks puzzled as he rocks back on his heels. "Undoubtedly, Fleming acted on the power of his best judgment."

"What are you saying?"

"I am saying that a man cannot die twice, both in the spring and in the summer. Somewhere there is a falsehood. Most likely with Fleming's record."

"Well." I am taken aback. An answer, but not the one I'd have wagered. "If there's a cover-up, my cousin Quinn knows more than he's telling."

Geist frowns. "Perhaps you should let sleeping dogs lie."

"Except that nobody is sleeping," I say. "Nobody is at rest. That's why I'm here. Mr. Geist, you said on my last visit that if you took my photograph it might help me commune with Will. And so I thought if we could take the photograph today, I'd have another chance—"

But he is tut-tutting me. "Your visit is ill timed, Miss Lovell. The photogenic process is a recipe of art and science. There's not enough light today. Exposure would be interminable."

Geist must see my disappointment. "Stay for tea," he says. "Though it's not a perfect day for a photographic portrait, I have several sheets of albumen paper drying in my darkroom. Perhaps in an hour or so the clouds will have broken up. And then," he says, with another dubious glance at Will's letter before he folds it and returns it to my hand, "we shall see what we shall see."

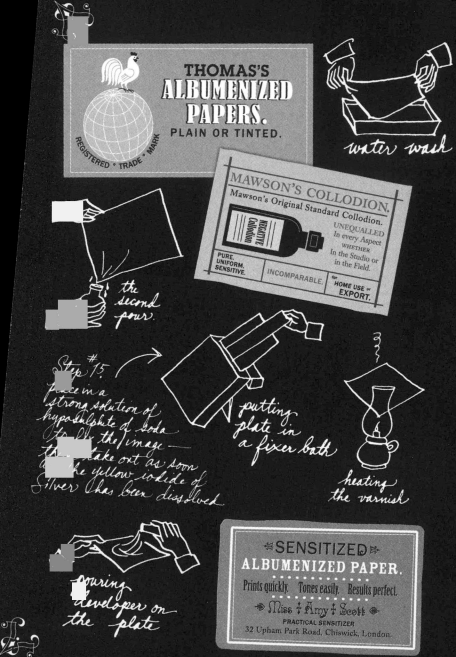

17.

"Light destroys the image. But light also creates the image."

Geist explains this carefully, as he has been explaining everything. I hardly want to blink, I am so fascinated. It is akin to a glimpse inside the magician's top hat, or a peek inside P. T. Barnum's museum.

After a desultory meal of Swiss cheese, sliced pickles, cranberry nut bread, and strong Ceylon tea, Geist had thrown open the velvet curtains of his studio and risked the dubious noonday light to take my photograph. The exposure time had crawled on longer than one of Reverend Meeks's Sunday sermons. And even in church I am allowed a scratch or two.

But I'd kept calm as marble. Chin lifted, hands folded. I had filled my mind with Will. Worked with all my power to recapture that surge of his presence, the undertow as I'd first known it that day in Geist's sitting room. Only there was nothing. No feverish heat. No fury. No pull.

My intense concentration had its own effect. When Geist capped the lens, I was weak with yearning. Geist seemed to understand, for after he'd removed the plate, he gave me his handkerchief before hurrying off to his darkroom. "Find me when you're ready."

Curiosity dried my tears, and soon I had followed him to the tiny chamber off the parlor where he worked. Its windows are papered against the light, and the trapped air is sharp with chemical solution. I watch as Geist prepares to develop the plate by pouring a vinegar solution over it and then waiting for the image to appear. "Developing a photograph is chemically similar to rubbing the tarnish off silver," he explains. "A scrub for the treasure beneath." Geist pours water over the plate.

"And both processes leave blackened hands."

"Indeed. Some even call photography the 'black art.'"

"I like that." But in my photograph I look grim and grainy. I'm not sure what we're hoping to find, but I don't dare ask Geist. Not while he is working so intently. He slides the plate into a wooden box.

"Fixer…to preserve the image." He leaves it for a few minutes to bustle about, selecting from a distracting array of bottles filled with a sharp bite of chemicals before removing the plate and washing it again with water.

Geist holds the plate over an oil lamp. "The varnish adheres best when the plate is warmed." He tips the glass this way and that. "I've used a Rapid Rectilinear portrait lens, a gift from Locke. I did sense a sharpened focus when I adjusted the aperture opening. But the proof of the pudding is in the eating."

He warms the plate a few more minutes before returning to his worktable, where he unstoppers a decanter and flows a thin solution onto the plate's surface.

"You added that liquid to the plate before you placed it in the camera," I mention.

"Not quite. That was collodion—a combustible blend of ether, io-dides, bromides, plus a bit of my own magic." He winks. "Collodion on the front. Then a bath of silver nitrate. Both compounds sensitize the plate before exposure. But we're finished with exposure."

"What are you pouring?" I sniff. It stinks.

"Varnish, to preserve the picture. It's a delicate balance. Too much varnish destroys. Whereas too little will not protect."

There are more steps to the process than in a Viennese waltz, and it requires such a mindful eye and steady hand that I feel shamed remembering how I'd dismissed Geist as a fraud and nothing else.

He is as skilled as a surgeon, but with his artist's eye I'm reminded of Will, who would have found astonishing artistry in this process.

When Geist holds the varnished plate at arm's length, my heart flutters.

"But I look…"

"Like a ghost? Not to worry, Miss Lovell; it's only the negative image. Not the finished print. Let's set it here until it dries. Meantime, there are some other things I want to show you."

Photographs
from
M. Geist

It seems wrong
to prey on the
Fragile Hopes
of the Bereaved.

18.

After propping up my plate, Geist leads me to his photographic archives kept in the bottom drawer of the secretary in his darkroom.

Some of his models are posed. Others wear thick cloaks or the diaphanous gowns of angels. There are hazy, chain-dragging apparitions and crisply focused, hooded specters. Many models point into a far-flung distance. Several times I recognize Viviette.

"An ideal model," Geist acknowledges. "She can turn still as a Greek urn for minutes on a stretch, and she never complains. An unearthly quality, wouldn't you agree? I can never predict how she'll hold the light. Go on, take some." He hands me a small stack of photographs. "I have many copies."

I accept his offering, but I feel uneasy all the same. Any business that looks to profit from death just couldn't be entirely honorable. When I mention that I'd like to see what Locke has brought back from his travels, Geist agrees with reluctance.

In the foyer he unbuckles the satchel and pulls out a heavy stack of glass plates. "As I'd feared. The images are cracked, scratched, chipped. Some are ruined altogether."

"The surfaces are dirty," I notice. "I don't know what I'm looking at."

"These are ambrotypes. Underdeveloped negatives. To be seen, they need to be mounted on a black background. But indeed they are dirty. Locke used a portable darkroom, and he often worked out in the field. Not the most sanitized conditions. Let's take these to the pantry. I shall see about restoring them at a later time."

Entering, I see that Geist has converted his pantry into a storage room of prints and files, with shelves of cloudy glass beakers, labeled bromide jars, and wooden plate holders.

"Where do you keep your china? Your housekeeper must be at her wit's end."

"Truth be known, there is no china—nor housekeeper," Geist admits. "Though Viviette is handy at whipping up a frothy egg-white solution for my albumen prints. She's indispensable to me. Her illness has created a void in my work."

"I hope she's better soon."

Geist's hands close into tight fists. "And I hope the scalawag who's got her into such a fix will make an honest woman of her," he says. "If this is indeed what she wants. Whatever the solution, I'm hopeful that she'll return to work as soon as possible. Make no mistake, it is Viviette who has the touch. She is indispensable to my practice." And while I am surprised by all this news, I have no doubt that Geist's agitation is sincere.

When we revisit the darkroom, I prickle with anticipation. "I'm a ghost," I say softly.

"Indeed. But we print in the other room, in as much sunlight as we can find." And now I am introduced to the printing process as

Geist places the plate and a sheet of paper into a wooden printing frame. "Come with me."

Back through to the dining room, Geist draws the curtain and sets the frame in the windowsill to absorb the wash of beryl-yellow sun peeking from behind the winter clouds.

"We must wait another five minutes for the image to print onto the paper. After toning and fixing, it will turn a rich shade, something between chocolate and eggplant." But Geist's energy is gone. His face sinks like a misbegotten soufflé as he checks the frame. "Alas, thus far the print and negative are alike as a pair of kidneys. For a moment I'd suspected we might have had another Du Keating on our hands."

"Du Keating?"

"A story for another time."

"Please, tell it now. I want to hear." I can't leave, not now, with nothing to show for my visit but my plain and ordinary likeness.

Geist has been eagle-eyed on my print image, but I sense that he doesn't find what he wants. His gaze flicks up to hold mine through the darkness. "For that sort of story we'll need my fire and my scotch. And then, Miss Lovell, you must go. It's not appropriate for a young lady to be out and about so late."

I touch the edges of the print. "May I take this when it's dried?" Though the picture doesn't flatter me, I like that I am posed alone. No Aunt Clara simpering at my elbow.

"With my blessing."

Out of the darkroom, I see through the window that snow is beginning to fall. It's getting late, but the idea of returning to Pritchett House after this afternoon of magic depresses me. Only Mavis knows where I am and had agreed to fib that I'm in bed with a sick headache, should anyone inquire.

In his sitting room, Geist prods at the logs with his toaster iron then pours himself a scotch and offers me a glass of apple brandy, which I take.

The liquid rolls warm down my throat and erases the sticky tang of photographic chemicals that had been lingering in my nose and lungs.

Geist takes the tumbler of scotch and then settles deep into his wingback chair. As if he wants to surround himself in light and comfort before he lets his mind move backward into darker matters.

Pritchett House, Brookline, Mass.

HEINRICH GEIST

MEDIUM AND PHOTOGRAPHER

Tremont Street
Boston, Massachusetts

the house
is Ugly
UGLY, and
Cold

the
picture
doesn't
flatter.

19.

I first learned of the Du Keating affair when I was living in Paris. I'd been studying photography back in the forties under the great Disderi," begins Geist. "It was he who told me this tale of a wealthy Parisian couple whose young daughter, Marie-Claire, had come down with a fever that took a violent turn for the worse. When she died, she left her parents absolutely shocked and heartbroken.

"In this same family was an older brother, Aurelian, who could neither read nor write and was bereft of even the slightest social grace. Aurelian did not attend school, and his parents hardly bothered with him. He was, however, enormously interested in photography. Which in those days, Miss Lovell, was only a burgeoning scientific art, nothing like what it has become today.

"Aurelian du Keating had been close with his sister, and after her death he claimed that she haunted him. He began to suffer from violent night terrors. The story goes that as the boy mastered his hobby, he began to obsessively photograph his deceased sister's empty bed. On days when there was no light and he could not work the camera, he curled up in her bed and slept."

"Did he allow anyone to see his finished photographs?"

Geist shakes his head. "Not at first. As soon as he had developed a daguerreotype, the boy secreted it back to his rooms. Frankly, nobody was much interested in his activities. After all, where is the intrigue in photographing an empty bed? Or so they thought. But Aurelian's nightmares became so tortured, and his habits so fanatical, that eventually his work was uncovered and brought forth. And what a horrible shock when they beheld it."

A log splits, shooting a scatter of sparks up the flue and a tremor up my spine. No fire can warm me at this moment. "Faint at first, the image became clearer with each plate," Geist continues. "There in the photograph was the image of Marie-Claire's corpse. Not as she'd lain angelic on her pillow, but in a state of grotesque decomposition. It was," he says with a sigh, "most horrific."

I swallow. The back of my mouth is dry as dust. "What happened next?"

"The household went into an uproar. It was as much a proof of haunting as any had ever reckoned with. Most of the servants fled. Hex symbols were branded into the doors. There was a failed attempt to torch the Du Keating chateau. Cursed by the devil, they said it was. Better to burn it down.

"The girl's body, which had been interred in the family crypt, was removed and reexamined. When the physician suspected foul play, young Aurelian confessed. Apparently he'd so believed in the magical power of photography that he'd prepared a solution of the same ingredients used to prepare the photographic plates and administered it to his sister. He had tried, as he most pitifully explained, to cure his beloved Marie-Claire of her fever." Geist's eyes search the firelight. "Instead, he had killed her."

Horror twists inside me. "Mr. Geist, did *you* see any of these images?" Though I can see the answer in his face.

Almost imperceptibly Geist's face hardens. "Unfortunately, I did. Disderi managed to obtain one," he admits. "Poison had distorted the girl's features, and her flesh was a paste over her skeleton. And her eyes. Stuck wide open." Momentarily he closes his own. "Eternal in her last moments. Though I would do anything to not have seen it, from that moment I was a believer."

"In what?"

"In Marie-Claire du Keating. And in William Pritchett. I believe in the spirit afterlife. The dead are here, all around us."

A chilling thought. "Whatever happened to Aurelian?"

"His end is not so tragic. After his confession it was decided Du Keating needed special care, and he was placed in a monastery near Languedoc. It's said he lives there, quite contentedly, to this day. His sister's spirit did more good than harm. Which is as Marie-Claire would have wanted it and doubtless why she made contact. She loved her brother—despite his terrible crime. She knew he was bedeviled by an unsound mind and that he needed more attention than what her parents could provide. She wanted him safe."

I lean forward in my chair, my hands gripping the glass. "Mr. Geist, why do you think Will needs to contact me?"

The photographer sits back. "It could be any number of reasons." He ticks them off with his fingers. "Perchance Pritchett wants to send a warning, or expose a truth, or make a confession. Or perhaps he simply needs to remind you of his pain and suffering."

"Why wouldn't he appear to me in a dream?"

"A dream? Bah." Geist flicks off my thought like water from his fingertips. "Dreams are nonsense, a cluttered attic of the

unconscious. You see, Miss Lovell, while most spiritualist photography is bunk, it can be a portal. Whether through photographs or séances, this is the pact that we make in this trade as we go about our daily business. We must respect those moments when a soul from the other side decides to rap on the door." Suddenly his fist knocks the underside of the mantelpiece.

I jump, hand to my heart. Then smile weakly. "Answering that door would frighten me."

Geist thinks. "*Not* to answer would frighten me," he parries, "for I am convinced that our beloved want the best for us."

I mull on this. "Mr. Geist, aside from communication through a medium, is there any other way I could connect somehow with the departed?"

"Why, of course. The oldest way of all." Geist rises from his chair and extends his hand to pull me to my feet. "If a soul has been accepted by God, then your prayer will be heard in His house."

"In church, you mean?"

"I mean in any consecrated space." He opens his arms. "Spiritualism is not just a trade. It is a religion. A vision of the Divine. Now, please excuse me. The hour is too late, and you must go. Let me paste a backing onto your print."

Later, though, it is not the comfort of church but the image of Marie-Claire's waxen face staring cave-eyed from her pillow that sears itself to my mind as I hurry along Aubrey Lane. The hackney that Geist had summoned and paid for has dropped me a little ways from Pritchett House so that I can steal home quietly on foot.

Last week, when I'd returned from the Black Iris, I'd been lucky that no one caught me slipping inside. Tonight, armed with the knowledge that Uncle Henry won't be making a late night return and that Mavis will vouch that I was tucked up in my attic bed, I'm not all that worried, until I catch sight of the house itself.

What an ugly house it is. The architecture is pretentious for Brookline, where genteel folk prefer a quieter façade. Its windows are ornate and as heavy as a dowager aunt. Its many columns are obtrusive. When I'd thought I might be the next Mrs. Pritchett, its faults seemed insignificant compared with its offer of shelter and love. But that was then.

Once inside, in the pantry, I tuck a bit of tea cake into a napkin— Geist and I had forgotten all about a proper supper—but as I pass through to the kitchen, an obstacle.

Mrs. Sullivan, who'd been sleeping in her chair by the hearth, is awake all at once and snarling like a cur. "You, there! Where've you been?"

"Oh…" But she has stumbled to a stand and in the next moment is much too close, her stale ale breath in my face. I draw back.

"Jezebel!" She thumps her knuckles against my shoulder, knocking me back. "Not even out of weeds yet, and look at you! Rushing off into the city, arranging secret meetings. He'll never do right by you, whoever he is, if that's the shameful plan you're hatching. Those sort of cads never—"

"Mrs. Sullivan, you're wrong—"

"Don't ever say I din't warn you! And now I'll have you know, tomorrow it'll be my sunrise duty to tell the Missus."

The very idea of being reported to Aunt for a crime I didn't commit infuriates me. My face burns and my hands clench, though my answering voice could cut glass. "Report all you like, Mrs. Sullivan. That's all Aunt Clara needs to turn me out. But what will you do without me? You tell me to be a lady—but does a lady beat carpets or polish silver? Does a lady sleep in a garret?"

In the next second I think Mrs. Sullivan might cuff my ear, a talent for which she is notorious. Instead, she glares, but then she steps back to let me pass. I keep my chin set proud, though I stiffen to feel her eyes following me.

Alone upstairs in my room, I turn the lock and sink to my knees. The fire I'd built earlier this evening has died, and my hands tremble so violently with anger and cold that it takes time to light a match. I hardly know why I bother. Warmth never holds in this room. It is as if the walls themselves prefer the chill.

At least tonight the atmosphere matches my mood. How vile to be accused—especially by Mrs. Sullivan, whose dimpled face had been some comfort when Mother's memory feels particularly faint or when Aunt is being loathsome.

The fire catches and blazes. And now I hear the housekeeper's own lumpish foot on the stairs and the rusty hinges of her door as she retires.

It's not entirely Mrs. Sullivan's fault that she croaks and spits at me. The housekeeper uses the same coarse and casual manner not only with Mavis and Lotty, but also with the neighbors' servants. And while I'm not paid a wage, there is no real distinction between the staff and me. Not anymore. My clothes are thread-worn. The strongest lye can't rid the half-moons of garden dirt from under my nails or the stink of cod from my palms. My days are filled with chores. I don't entertain, nor do I receive invitations to be entertained. I am not the lady of this house. Never was. Certainly never will be.

The cord of my purse strings has wound itself tight around my wrist, cutting into my flesh with a sudden fierce intensity, the way

Toby and I used to pinch each other to stop ourselves from laughing in church.

But this is hardly humorous, for I can feel the welt rise on my skin.

Hurriedly, I work the strings loose and pull it open. The cry dies in my throat.

It is as if Will's own hand has squeezed hold of my heart. And as if to confirm it, the fever is upon me at once, the memory of his rage so pure it strikes me to my marrow as I stare at the photograph.

You led
me to my
locket, Love.
But how?

20.

The full moon won't lie. In a rush, I bring the print to the window. My eyes aren't playing tricks. The photograph has changed. Black ink is scratched at my breastbone. A crooked little heart. No prank, no forgery. The print has been in my bag since leaving the studio.

The fever of Will's anger has passed through me and is gone, leaving me wilted. Despite the cold, my hairline beads with sweat. I crawl into a corner of the sill and offer my ignited cheeks, one and then the other, like hot kisses against the frosted pane, before I compose myself enough to return my gaze to the photograph.

I lick my fingers and rub. The ink is indelible. Furthermore, I know exactly what it means. "I believe in you," I whisper to the darkness beyond. "I know you've come back to me." And I do know it. Rarely have I been so sure of anything.

My breath has turned the glass opaque, and I wipe away the fog to stare outside, far across the lawn. The tree isn't visible from my vantage point, and fresh snow is dropping, thick and fast as rain. I want to leave this instant, but I must be sure the house is asleep. The last thing I need is Mrs. Sullivan catching me again.

My bones seem to vibrate under my skin as I draw up my legs and twine my arms around my knees. I am so quiet that a mouse darts across the carpet and stakes its claim to a bit of tea cake crumb that had dropped from my napkin.

A spy must know when and how to turn to stone.

A thousand years pass before I hear snoring proof that Mrs. Sullivan is lost to the sleep of the overworked.

Creeping along the corridor, I freeze at the sound of Mavis muttering in her bed. But no, she's only dreaming. It turns my heart imagining what rebuke had been meted at Mrs. Sullivan's ready hand once she'd discovered I wasn't home and that Mavis had been lying to her.

Dear Mavis, she's lost half her hearing to Mrs. Sullivan's punishing blows, and yet when I press her she'll swear one more knock doesn't matter. I'll have to think of a way to make it up to her.

Outside, the snow sticks four inches deep and continues to fall. In seconds my head and shoulders and back are wet. Hesitant to use the lantern, I let the watery moonlight guide me down the lawn. Almost immediately I'm soaked from my slipping, skidding shoes. My feet are two numb chunks of ice wrapped in soggy wool, and there's hardly any point in lifting my dragging hem, though it seems to catch on every twig. My dress is all but ruined, but nothing could turn me back now. My photograph has given me hope, and I will doggedly cast my last coin in its wishing well.

A spy advances on every opportunity.

The butternut tree marks an otherwise desolate part of the property. Its branches haven't been climbed in many years. Its knotted rope swing is too frayed and thin to support a body. But it's not the swing that interests me.

At the base of the tree I drop down to all fours. My blind hands search and find the nicks and grooves where we have carved our initials: *T. P. L.*, Tobias Pritchett Lovell. *W. F. P.*, William Franklin Pritchett. *Q. E. P.*, Quincy Emory Pritchett. *J. R. L.*, Jennie Rose Lovell.

And then, two summers ago, Will had taken his fishing knife and joined his initials with mine, fencing them together inside a single, exuberant heart. I see it now, cut thick like an artery into the wood's black bark, shaped like a spade with a kited tail.

An identically shaped heart has been inked into my photograph.

The heart that marks the spot.

My hands crawl at the patch of soft soil directly beneath the heart, at the wedge that divides the tree's two largest exposed roots. I can feel that the earth has been turned over recently. My breath is short, my hands scrape like a dog, raw, burrowing. Grit flies into my eye. I wipe at it, streaking more wet dirt across my face and lips. It leaves an icy taste of mineral. Tomorrow it will be impossible to explain away the state of my clothes and shoes. But I cannot stop until I have found what William has intended me to find.

The physical sensation of pulling it up is not unlike the complicated pull on the tangle of a winter root loosing its grip in the ground. As if it, too, had been connected to the earth and sustained by it.

Even though I know what it is, a small sound escapes me, a euphoria trickling through the flood of my grief. A knowledge that calms me.

My frost-blunted fingers wind through the chain. My necklace, my locket. Returned.

BlackBErry

cMerry

STRAWBERRY

Our benefactors migh[t] [tur]n Us, or Turn Us ou[t] [a]t any givin Moment

ALWAYS BE RESORCE[F]U[L]

a SPy must watch for aLL Opshuns a[n]

A SPy can OPen Whatever is Locked.

21.

Snow has muffled the outside world, but sunshine eventually starts a gurgle down the drainpipe outside my window. I wake blinking and see that Mavis has already visited my room and taken my ruined dress to salvage. What's more, the floorboards have been wiped clean of my footprints, my water pitcher is freshly filled. A washcloth hangs on its hook beneath the basin. Pleats knife-creased and collar starched, my Sunday dress is draped over my chair, and my boot buckles are shined and ready for church.

Back in my room last night, I'd tucked my locket beneath my mattress. This morning I pull it out and rinse off the encrusted grit before I dry the necklace link by link. Then I fasten the clasp around my neck and tuck both chain and locket inside my collar, out of sight.

Quinn must have brought home the necklace after all. Whatever his reasons for burying it, I need to find him. I have to hear his story whole, and not just in the pieces that I've stitched into a quilt of guesswork. No matter how much he wants to protect Will, his silence conjures up the worst of my imagination. Nothing Will had done could be so bad that I can't endure it.

Mavis is clearing the breakfast things when I appear in the doorway of the empty dining room. "Where is Quinn? Where are my aunt and uncle?"

She freezes, a platter balanced in each hand. "Good morning, Miss. I believe they decided to set off without you."

"Services don't start until a quarter past eight. Why've they gone already?"

"Oh, I can't say, Miss." But Mavis's gaze drops.

"Was Mrs. Sullivan unkind to you last night?" I ask. "No, don't answer, for I know she was. I'm very sorry, Mavis. I'm in your debt."

"Wasn't anything that hasn't happened a hundred times before, Miss," she murmurs. Somehow it is the routine of cruelty that seems a worse offense to me than the recent blow Mavis surely suffered at Mrs. Sullivan's hand.

"Things will get better, I'm sure of it," I promise.

Mavis nods. She looks more wobblingly upset than usual.

"What is it?"

With the barest of movements, she jerks her head toward the front door. "They are just leaving now, Miss," she whispers. "Go catch 'em outright."

A spy must retain at least one loyal alliance.

I tear down the hall and through the front door just in time to see the carriage turning. Without pausing to think, I dash out to step in front of it, slipping on the shoveled ice and bringing the driver to a cursing stop.

We exchange a look, and then he relents with a small nod, letting me run around to the side to jump onto the foot step and rap my fist against the carriage window. Uncle opens the door, allowing Aunt to lean across him so that she might make excuses for them both.

"Such a ruckus, Jennie!" Aunt's face is so close that I see the ash of burnt match she uses to darken the gray in her brows and the talcum powder that cakes the pores of her nose and ringed crinkles of her neck. The lie of her smile tenses her lips.

"Why are you leaving for church without me?"

"I thought we'd discussed this." Into my stony silence, she continues. "When all is said and done, Jennie, you aren't Episcopalian." Aunt sniffs, gaining confidence. "In fact, your father, if I recall correctly, was *Universalist*." Aunt speaks this word as if she has called my father a heathen. "Mr. Pritchett and I thought you might want to join his old congregation today. It might be a sure fit, we hoped, with your background and beliefs."

But I understand the implication at once. Aunt and Uncle don't want me to attend church with them. They don't want to appear in public with me, as their ward. I look to Uncle Henry, who is scrutinizing his watch face.

"That's fine, then," I respond calmly. "I'll find my own way to church. But aren't you forgetting Quinn?"

Aunt Clara's smile curdles. "Rather, Quinn is forgetting us. He's nowhere to be found, and I'm sure Reverend Meeks will inquire after him. It's really quite embarrassing, and rather a snub, besides. If you see him, Jennie, please inform him that if he didn't want to go church, he had only to tell us." Aunt seems entirely unaware, as she clamps the door shut, that in attempting to sneak off to church without me, she has snubbed me in the exact same way.

When I reenter the house, the absolute quiet is disconcerting. I run to the back of the house and downstairs to the kitchen, still warm with the aroma of soda-bread biscuits, which Mrs. Sullivan bakes every Sunday at dawn. When I call out, my voice reverberates lonely through the passage. No answer. So the servants, too, have left me behind. While Mrs. Sullivan has not—yet?—reported to Aunt my trespasses of last night, she is making her disdainful point and dragging poor Mavis along behind her.

"No matter." It's a mile walk to First Parish. I'll sit in a pew by myself.

But it does matter. The silence in the house feels reproachful.

Any consecrated space, Geist had said. Surely First Parish is as consecrated as any other church.

Upstairs, my Bible rests on the hall table by the coat closet. As I approach, my step is stern as a schoolmistress, and I'm bothered with a sensation that I'm not all alone here after all. Like an object that is in sight but briefly, a shimmer caught in the corner of an eye, the sound is faint. A shift. A whisper. And then, more clearly, I hear smothered laughter.

The echo of my footfall dies. I approach with caution. The sound has come from behind the closet door—the very same hideaway spot where Toby and I'd whiled away the hours when we wanted to be alone. In the darkest corner, we'd hidden notes to each other; jokes and riddles and Rules for Spies, folded beneath the jars of strawberry and plum preserves that we'd devour, scraping to the bottom—the treat made all the sweeter for being stolen out of Mrs. Sullivan's pantry. Even after my twin's death, I've come upon his notes to me folded and wedged into the closet's floorboards. It is as if Toby knew, even then, what the future held. As if he was training me.

"Who's there?" I grasp the doorknob and pull. And pull again, more forcefully, rattling the knob. Odd. There's no way to lock the door from inside. The hinges must be stuck.

Behind the door, silence. But a resonant silence, the kind that holds the air after the final note of a concerto has been played. In my mind's eye, I see myself and Toby huddled among the cloaks and galoshes, my teeth chewing at my knuckles as Toby used both hands to keep a firm grip on the knob before sitting back with a victorious *haw!* once the servant on the opposite side had given up.

But I'm on this side of the cupboard. Not that side.

"Open up!" I call. I stamp my foot and kick the door, scuffing it, to no avail. "Who's in there? Tell me! For I can hear you!" I'm nearly wrenching the doorknob from its plate. My palms are slick, my mind wheels to steady me, to find the logic. Lotty's little sister, perhaps? Or one of those innumerable Hodge children from down the road, sneaking out of Sunday school?

Yet now the quality of silence has changed. Emptied. Gone. I release my hold. Stand and rub my eyes with the heels of my hands.

I'm dizzy. I feel a sudden melting in the core of my body, an itch in my eyes when I blink.

My unexpected reunion with my necklace and the turmoil of the past few days have all wound me up too tight. Nothing darker than my imagination is hiding in that closet. The door sticks sometimes. Especially when it hasn't been opened in a while.

I step back, done with it, but then pull the door in one last, vigorous wrench. It swings open with a creak that sounds like a laugh at my efforts. The new weightlessness behind the handle trips me off balance.

"Hello?" I call.

Nothing. There's nothing inside the closet but winter wraps— and the heavy smell of camphor.

HARPER'S WEEKLY

JANUAR

THE SCOUT

26

A VOICE FROM ANDERSONVILLE.
a poem.

"Sick, and in prison."
Poor Tom's just gone ! I closed his eyes.
He died in muttering low the text That says, "They never hunger more."
I lie and w̶o̶n̶d̶e̶r who'll go next
So r̶ ̶ ̶ ̶ ̶ ̶ ̶ ̶ ̶
doo̶
Oh̶
ma̶
hu̶
Co̶
gra̶
Hol̶
It w̶ ̶ ̶ ̶ ̶ hell-f̶ ̶ ̶ ̶ ̶ ̶ll
brai̶
coul̶
Onc̶
cour̶
Did̶
Whe̶
dear̶
Hur̶
rag̶
me back? Stand by the 2̶d̶ ̶R̶e̶
Wh̶

I had a dream. Oh help! Be quick! Come mother, Ruth! (Don't say I died
With Tom, poor Tom ! dead by my side.) Who says, "I was in prison sick,
And yet ye came not unto lie."
"I was athirst, and hungered too." Ah then He knows our agony ! Read, Jack, how cunning Satan ̶ ̶ ̶ ̶ ̶ ̶ ̶ ̶ ̶ ̶ ̶ ̶ ̶
Hurrah ! I'll fight while there's a rag. Off boys ! why do you keep me back? Stand by the old Red, White, and Blue !
Ah, is it death? I can not see!

until I'd raised a baud
Who'd vow with steadfast heart and hand To dare and die until we'd broke Their prison-doors and set them free.

But, Jack, no matter ! We won't flinch From death by starving, if the Lord
Do su er this. But this I know !
I'd slay my country's deadly foe In honest battle with my sword, But not in prison, inch by inch.
Oh, Jack, come close ! I'm going fast ! If you get home tell mother this:
before the thousands die !"

ARTIFICIAL LEGS
& ARMS SEPLPHO'S PATEN

SO-CALLED "CURTIS'S RAIDERS" IN THE PRISON AT CAMP SUMTER AWAITING EXECUTIV
SKETCHED BY AN ENGLISH ARTIST.—[SEE PAGE 17.]

it was in the
country of Ea
evening was gro
camp-fire was
and lower, but w
for the spell of
ous gift of sto
none of us w
Captain Char
been a Lieuten
Battery at the
the war, but
excitement and
had early pro
employment a
he soon rose t
He is a man
well educated
inventive bra
about to relate
tion of it as it
if there is aug
diction as her
̶ ̶ ̶ ̶ ̶ ̶ ̶ ̶ sly
̶ ̶ ̶ the ruddy
̶ ̶ g camp-fire
̶ ̶ g over his
̶ elligent face,
̶ hair waving
̶ wind, which
̶ ̶ from the
̶ hillier.
̶ rn Virginia,
̶ personally
̶ ommander,
̶ the war
̶ g intimated,
̶ the date of
̶ to try my
̶ service–of
̶ equired to
̶ llas with
̶ rly teemed
̶ ate in the
̶ lighted to
̶ rt at his
̶ ral was a instruc-
̶ y reliable
̶ ̶ ̶ worth) was killed last
̶ t the lower ford; and
F. (the rebel commander)
ead-quarters at the Sedley
on the (CONTINUED)

22.

I see them as soon as I'm around the bend on Cypress. Beyond the spire of First Parish, beyond the snowy lawn of the old burying ground, a cluster of mourners has gathered around a fresh grave. Even considering the weather, this funeral seems paltry. I pause a moment to watch before I continue into the church.

Though Aunt Clara flung it as an accusation and is too much of a goose to know if it's true or not, she is correct. My father was an Universalist. When he was alive, we occasionally attended services. I feel more lapsed than blasphemous, though, as I enter First Parish, where I slide into a pew in back. But this morning I crave something different from prayers and hymns. I need the breath of Will's spirit. I need him before me. My heart aches with hope.

I open my Bible to my selected passage. My lips silently mouth the words of the ancient prayer. "Grant, O Lord, to Thy servant departed, that he may not receive in punishment the requital of his deeds. May Thy mercy unite him above to the choirs of angels."

I've slid both of Geist's prints into the book to mark the page. Viviette's crown of irises and the heart on my breastbone are Will's communication in plain sight. "I forgive any crimes you've committed, Will," I whisper, "and I promise that I'll wear my neck-lace always, to honor our love and your memory. I'm glad you led my way to it." There.

From my perch at the edge of the pew, I watch the drift of dust motes caught in the sunbeam through the stained-glass windows. It is mesmerizing, light and dust creating a reminder that God's beauty is all around us.

I've been so eager for a sign. The fever again. The undertow. Nothing comes. After a few minutes I allow myself a peek around me. The faces of the congregation are hard in their unfamiliarity, and the air feels strained with other peoples' fervor. We worship in unison, but our troubles are all our own.

Why did I think Will would be here? Will, who preferred a Sunday picnic to a Sunday service. Disappointment eddies through me. How stupid, really, to believe that church was a consecrated space for him. My attention falters through the rumble of the ser-mon, the recitations, prayers, and song. Will is like a dream just out of my reach.

A final processional hymn and the service is over. I'm first to go. Outside, walking under the dripping yews, I see mourners trudging back from the burial. Among them I see Wigs, the barkeep from the Black Iris.

I stop and shade my eyes to get a better look. Though protected by the hood of his mackintosh, Wigs feels my watch on him. He looks up, his fish mouth agog, as I dart to the cemetery gates.

"Eh. Didn't even bother to pay a last regard? Least you might've done." He grasps the top of the gate and knocks the toe of one boot and then the other against the iron rail to dislodge the snow. "Though the boy said you weren't his Frances, after all, he called you a friend. 'Tain't much of one, in my eyes. Got your servant girl to send a chicken soup, and a call from your fancy doctor, who couldn't do no more for him than our own Norris. So I guess your conscience is clean."

"That burial was Private Dearborn's?"

"Don't play innocent with me, Miss." Wigs shakes a handkerchief from his pocket and blows his nose wetly into it.

"I didn't…" I stare across to the farthest, snowy reach of the cemetery, bordered by pines. A lone figure stands at the grave.

Even from that far away, I can see that it's Quinn.

"He went quick." A harried young woman, her hair half-unbundled and her face tinged with cold, has come to stand next to Wigs. A child clinging behind her wipes his nose on her skirts. "He came down with fever Tuesday morning, died Friday, and was buried today." She looks kinder than her father. She turns to him now. "Best to hurry, Fa. I've got the stew on."

"Are you the one who cared for Nate?" I ask.

"I am. I'm Sue." When she smiles, shyness turns her face even rosier.

"Not that it makes a whit of difference to you," Wigs adds in his blunt, bullying way, "who didn't share that burden at all."

"I'm sorry, but I didn't really know him." I catch my breath and then say, awkwardly, "My name is Jennie Lovell. Nate Dearborn was in the same regiment as my fiancé, William Pritchett. He was killed this summer in battle at the Wilderness, in Virginia. I hadn't met Nate until last week, but I'd like to pay my condolences to the boy's family all the same. Are they here?"

My words have caused Sue's eyes to round like an otter's, and I sense a change in Wigs's manner, too. "No, Miss, there's no family," she answers faintly. "We telegraphed to Pittsfield to notify his kin. Seemed he hadn't anyone close, though a cousin did telegraph back. 'Twas a most distressing communication. He'd thought the boy'd been dead for months. In fact, he'd had a captain's telegram this past summer that stated Nate had fallen in battle. In the Wilderness. Just like your William." She concentrates her stare on me, awaiting some clarification.

"The records of the fallen are sometimes painfully inaccurate," I note. But my mind is reeling. It's too much a coincidence.

"He'd been lucky to have died in battle," adds Wigs, whose disapproval toward me seems to have neutralized with my explanation. "Least it'd been over quick."

"Pyemia is the name the doctor gave it. An infection that got in Nate's blood after the amputations." Sue hoists the child to her hip. "Such suffering in that boy's short life."

I murmur sympathies, but then have to ask, "Did the cousin in Pittsfield give you the captain's name? The one who signed the death notice?"

Sue taps her fingers to her lips. "There was a name, but I can't recall."

"James Fleming, perhaps?"

"That's it, yes." Sue nods. "He was commander to your fiancé, too?"

"He was." Out of the corner of my eye, I watch Quinn exit the cemetery, skirting through to a shortcut that leads to the wooded trail back home.

"It's a forgiving commander who allows folk to think their boy fell on the field," says Wigs. "There's honor in it. For your fiancé, too, I'd warrant."

It is an almost audible click into place. Of course. In one powerful signature, Fleming bestowed legitimacy on the captured men of his company. The grace of a death in combat, so that families wouldn't suffer to learn the horror of death in prison. What did Nate say? *Slipped the noose.* Nate Dearborn was supposed to be dead. My stomach lurches. Quinn would never confess it, but he might confirm it.

First I'll need to catch up with him, though. Before he locks himself in his room or disappears for the rest of the day.

"Excuse me, then." To Sue, "Very glad to meet you." To Wigs, "Good day, sir." And I peel off as fast as my muddy boots can take me.

Quinn has kicked a path through the snow, which helps my own journey, but he has a lead by a few minutes. When I reach the bend and shout his name, I can feel him startle, though he keeps his pace.

"Where are you coming from?" He looks suspicious. "Are you spying on me?"

"Spying on you?" I try a laugh, which falters. "'Course not. Why would I be?"

He doesn't answer, but his answering scowl reminds me of a particular day, years ago, when Toby and I'd first arrived at Pritchett House. Exuberant, Will had taken me in hand at once, eager to show off all his home's delights—from Uncle's ivory menagerie to the lions carved in the parlor fireplace, and the Dresden jar where Aunt kept her digestive peppermints.

Quinn had followed from an aloof distance. Every moment we'd waited for him to turn his heel altogether. As if we were hunting him. "Best not to spy on cousin Quinn for a while," Toby had decreed in those early days. "His guard is high as ours." His guard is up now.

"I'm not spying at all," I promise. "But I saw you at Nate Dearborn's burial."

Quinn's silence speaks to his uncertainty.

"You were in the Twenty-eighth together," I continue. "In fact, you'd sent away a messenger a few weeks ago to prevent me from talking to him. But I found him anyway."

"However you know him, let me assure you, Dearborn wasn't fit for your company," Quinn retorts. "I'm paying for his tombstone as an anonymous gift, so he and I are square—but he wasn't welcome in Brookline. Not by me, anyway. He ought to have stayed on that train and gone all the way home." He pivots and starts to walk, but I won't let him outpace me.

"Nate was hiding something shameful from his family, and you know it. Stop lying, Quinn, it's no service to me—Will's letter confessed more than you'd ever want me to know."

He halts so suddenly that I almost career into him. He turns. Behind the steely freeze of his face lives the truth. I am sure of it.

"Will's letter?" he repeats. Is it fear that flickers in his eyes? Or is it something else?

"Yes. It told everything. That he and Nate were both prisoners of war, and both of them were sent to Camp Sumter." My words spill before I can catch them back. "Something happened to Will there, didn't it? He had no glorious death on the battlefield. He wasn't any hero. That's what Nate meant when he spoke about being the only one to slip the noose. Did Will commit some horrible crime while in prison? Was he…punished? Was Will hanged in prison?" I feel my lungs strain against the pressure of my corset as I voice my most shocking thought. "Quinn, was he?"

But he is shaking his head. "How did you get hold of that letter?"

"Nate gave it to me."

"This changes everything," Quinn says.

"It changes nothing," I protest. "Except that you can stop protecting Will. Please, tell me the truth."

"It's a deadly rotten, rotten business. I didn't think...I didn't realize you'd got hold of that letter." His voice is shaking.

"I understand that you're scared. None of us wants Will's name smeared. But I can't help re-piecing together from bits I've got when the whole picture doesn't make sense. And the less I know, the more it frightens me—especially when I'm sure that Will's spirit won't rest until the truth is laid bare. Geist himself has proved to me that it is fully possible for a restless soul to commune from beyond."

Quinn looks ashen, and I sense his reluctance to hear me out even as he waits for me to continue.

"I know that you're angry enough about whatever Will's done that you hid my necklace. It was you, wasn't it? But I found it anyway, see? He led me to it."

I draw out the locket and chain from beneath my collar. The winter light catches it. Quinn's gaze is pulled to the gold pendant as if hypnotized. "All right, Jennie," he answers after a pause, "if it's a confession you want. I didn't know what to do with it, so I...yes. I had it and I hid it. Just don't give me that Spiritualist bunk that you were *led*. Someone must have been spying on me from the house when I buried it." He flexes an eyebrow. "Most likely *you*, since you always seem to locate me easily enough."

It's no use trying to justify how I came to discover the locket. "The point is that it wasn't yours to hide."

Quinn thrusts the information at me quickly, as if he can't stand holding on to it anymore. "Actually, it *was* mine. Sometimes the truth laid bare is ugly. But here it is. My brother bet and lost your necklace in a card game."

"No." I draw back. The information is the lash of a horsewhip. "No, that's a lie."

"I wish it were. When I won it back some weeks later, I kept it." He shrugs, defiant. "Then when I came home, I couldn't give it to you. To see it 'round your neck would have been hypocrisy." His fists are solid at his sides. "Some things I won't abide."

I try to picture the soldiers' tent. The sputtering oil lanterns and empty whiskey bottles. Will at the poker table, slouched in his slatted chair, cards fanned to his chest, dangling the chain from his fingers before dropping it into the pot of coins and dented gimcracks. The sweat of suspense, then his good-natured laugh when he'd lost. It's an unnerving sort of image of a Will I'd never known.

"But that necklace has worth to me."

"I apologize. Guess I've never been much of a gentleman when I needed to be."

"You knew how I treasured it, you knew—" In a quick, choppy motion, Quinn's hand cups my chin as his kiss lands hard upon my mouth.

"Oh." My heart thumps with unladylike vigor. My desire—if that's what it is—frightens me. I pull away.

"Wear the damn necklace if you like," he says, his voice just above a whisper. "I didn't mean to kiss you. But it was the only thing I could think to do, to make you be quiet." He turns to go.

How can I think nothing of it when I am all afire? "Wait, Quinn. Wait."

He doesn't. I join him, my boots crunching along behind his as he forges the way. He hurries, but at one point he drags back the branch of an overhanging red maple so that I can duck beneath.

"You once spoke of defending the dead!" I call out. "What you couldn't have known is that Will comes to me in his own defense. He craves my forgiveness. And I would forgive him, Quinn. We all need our peace in order to move on."

Quinn glances over his shoulder, his eyes gleaming like a wolf's. "Is this more bunk from your communing with that fraud, Geist? I'm all for forgiveness, if that's where you're coming out. But the less said of Camp Sumter, the better. The truth would destroy my parents."

"You can't shrug off *everything* that you don't want to face." Though I'm unsure if I am referring to Camp Sumter or our kiss of a moment ago.

He stops walking, his posture losing some of its starch as his fingers press the temple of his bad eye. I can almost feel it throb myself.

"We *did* fight at the Wilderness, back in May," he supplies. "All of us—Dearborn, too. Dearborn was brazen but not a bad sort. But we lost more than half our company in Virginia, and it changed us. We were in a strange country, with death and horror all around. Soldiers stole food and bullets, fought with their fists, with knives—it wasn't long that some men of the company began to make alliances. It's one way to protect yourself. Watching one man's back and hoping he'll have yours. Will and Dearborn were thick. What happened after the two of them were captured I can't say firsthand. We got separated and I continued on to Savannah."

"Where you were wounded."

"Yes." He touches his eye reflexively. "Through runners, I learned Will and Dearborn had fallen in with another fellow, Charles Curtis."

"That name is familiar. It was in the letter."

"Curtis made the newspapers, too, though it wasn't much

reported—it didn't put us Yanks in so pretty a light. I have an article I can show you. Curtis spearheaded a gang of prisoners that called themselves Curtis's Raiders. A brutal bunch with murder in their hearts. I heard of one Raider who killed his own brother for a few dollars. Hid the corpse in a ditch and slept on top to hide the bones. Honest prisoners fought Raiders every day—a war inside a war—till orders came in from a Confederate general to get it stopped."

"You are telling me that...?"

"Yes, Jennie. Will was a Raider."

"'One broken neck, an example to others,'" I repeat the words of Will's letter.

"Six broken necks," Quinn corrects. "There was a trial in July. Where six men were hanged, including Curtis and Will. Somehow Dearborn paid off a jailer and escaped. Well, except they got him in the end."

In my mind's eye I see Will, steadfast in his military brass and buttons. The clean scent of Pears soap on his skin as he held me close and whispered his love, promising his heart and his safe return. My image is awash in light and hope and resists the shadow that is falling over it; that of a confused young man, ill prepared for the trials and darkness of war. Disenchanted, exhausted, witness to slaughter, and then a murderer himself. Did I ever know this Will? Do I sense him in the worried tug and rattle of my disturbed senses, as I try to press on without him?

Our conversation has drained us both. I sense that Quinn has retreated from me.

We walk until the roof of Pritchett House is visible beyond the trees. I hate the house on sight. Hate its monolithic walls and windows. If only I could have predicted what sorrows awaited me, I'd have fought like a dog before I passed through its doors.

"You were right, I should leave," I tell him. "There's nothing for me here."

I can't continue. Not one more step. But Quinn has stayed on my elbow.

"That's not true," he says, and the catch in his voice makes me look up. "I didn't kiss you back there to hush you, Jennie. I kissed you to be heard. I've wanted you to leave here for selfish reasons. My brother didn't deserve his death, but he didn't deserve you either."

Quinn's hand catches my fingers, which are so cold that it is only a pressure. I pause a moment, but when I step forward he pulls me in so tight his arms near wrap double around the small of my back. He falls against my body, and my hands slip around his neck as his head sinks to find purchase on my shoulder. The weight of his unburdening nearly crushes me. "I'll look after you now, Fleur," he whispers. "I promise. I will. If you think you can look after me?"

His flinted face is a map I've known since childhood. And yet my eyes have never traveled it so intently. Toby and I always thought that it was Quinn who was the cold one, holding himself apart from us. We judged him swiftly, as children do, without wisdom or compassion. Now I stare at this young man who has endured so much and has asked so little. Quinn's eyes are incandescent, guarded but hopeful.

"Of course I will, Quinn," I tell him. "You're all I have."

GODEY'S LADY'S BOOK

A B C

D E F

G H

I think this would look rather smart.

PLATE 31. JUNE 1864

And the softened heart of your man of snow
Shall bid the blue violets blossom below.
Oh, let us hope that time may bring
To earth some sweet and gentle spring,
When human hearts shall thaw, and when
The ice shall melt away from men;
And where the hearts now frozen stand,
Love then shall blossom o'er all the land!

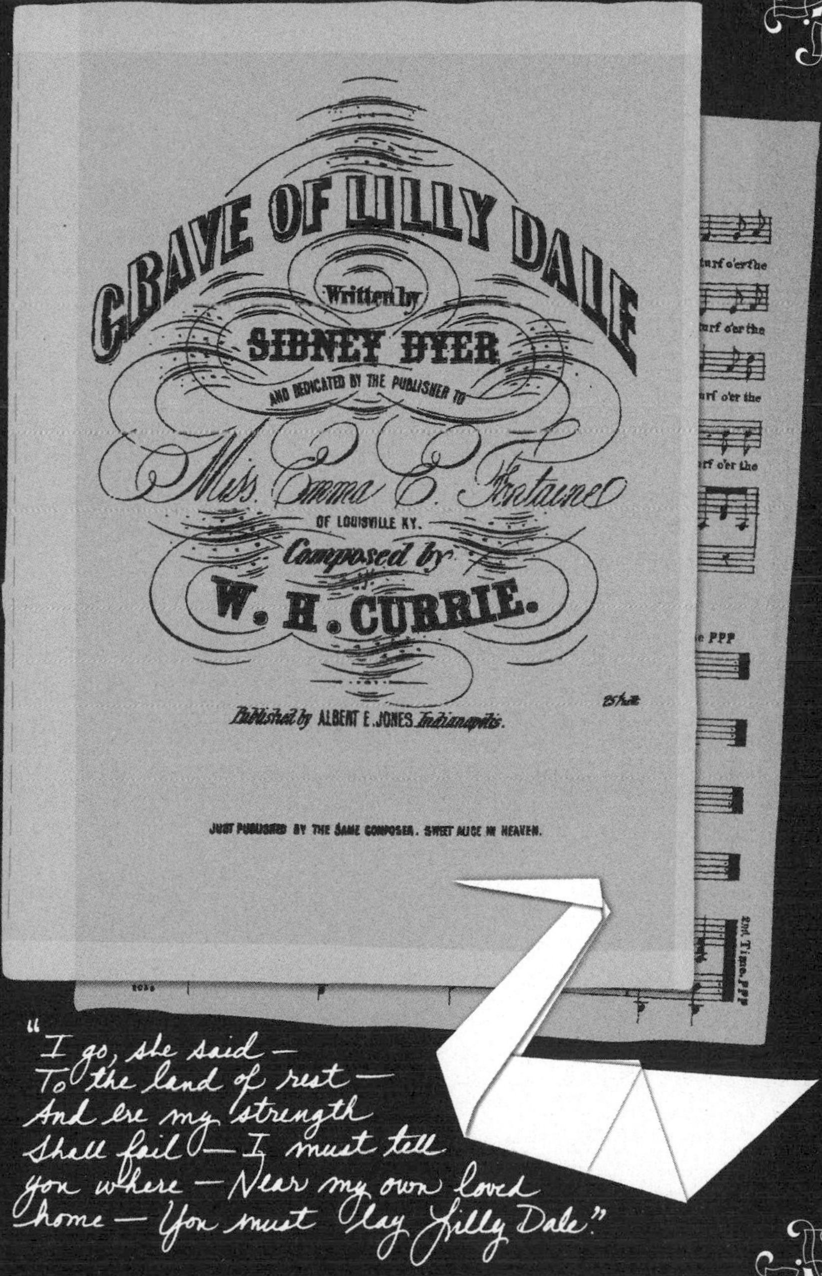

"I go, she said —
To the land of rest —
And ere my strength
shall fail — I must tell
you where — Near my own loved
home — You must "lay Lilly Dale"."

23.

We'd each left the house that morning alone, weighted by our private afflictions. Fingers laced and feet in step, we return to Pritchett House together. We have made a promise to each other, and our bond needs to be as strong as the stone and mortar that holds us here.

In a first act of faith, Quinn begins to collapse his smokescreens for me. He is relieved to show me the few articles on the Raiders that he has folded into brittle squares and slipped into the pages of his books. I secret one away for my scrapbook before advising him what to do with the rest.

"Dispose of these," I advise, and though I sense he cannot, I do have his ear on many other aspects of the household.

"You should take Mrs. Sullivan's key ring" is my first practical suggestion. "As long as she guards our cellar and larder, it is difficult to take inventory."

"That seems wise." And not a day later he presents me with the keys like a waggling retriever who has fetched a stick. It is not his only gift to me. One day I find a box of chocolate-covered almonds in my knitting basket. The next day it's a silky hair ribbon on my dresser. On my pillow that night is a poem clipped from the Atlantic Monthly, with a nosegay. Such devoted attentions and such a wealth of consideration after so little are an unbridled pleasure.

Still, the moments I wait for are not made of flowers and chocolates but our stolen, heated moments in the hall and at the banister, behind the library door, and once in the scullery, when Quinn sweeps me up so that only the tips of my toes touch the ground. His mouth hungry on mine as if seeking something extra, hidden, and secret, past my lips, my name whispered like some kind of elixir. What I had thought was arrogance I now know to be nothing but reserve, and not even much of that anymore.

"You won't leave me, will you, Fleur?" He often speaks this refrain into my ear as he presses against me.

"Never," I whisper back, so sure in my answer that I don't know why he continues to doubt and to ask.

I am no longer a spy. Toby's ghostly instructions were nothing but my own childish whims. I don't even care when Mavis shyly reports that she saw us kissing in the corridor.

"See? You'll be the Missus of the house yet, just as I always said," she declares. "Though I'm sorry to lose your company, Miss Jennie, it's the right order of things."

"As long as Mrs. Sullivan isn't boxing your ears. Now that I've got her precious keys, she's been in a foul temper."

Mavis shrugs, and I know that some things haven't changed.

To my face Mrs. Sullivan is all sullen deference. Re-affixing the *Miss* to my name and not so quick to serve me the burnt bits of toast or end pieces of meat. But I know that the housekeeper's resentment brews and that Mavis takes the brunt. There is nothing I can do. As long as Aunt Clara wields the official title of Mrs. Pritchett, Mrs. Sullivan's position here is all but guaranteed.

But I am gaining strength.

I put my past behind me. I salve my hands with cream twice a day to soften my calluses. Buff my nails and take time with my hair, twisting it into modern styles that I copy from a page in Aunt's *Godey's Lady's Book*. The day girls carry my washtub to my room again and fill it with steaming hot water and scented salts for my private bath. I don't protest. I want to look like a lady. For myself and for Quinn. His eyes on me sharpen my senses, and when he is near I feel my blush blooming, heat rising like spring sap in my blood after this long and harrowing winter.

At Quinn's urging, nights at Pritchett House take on a compatible pattern. Uncle at his desk while Aunt picks her butterfingers over her crewel and Quinn and I sit at the card table, where he teaches me gin, rummy, and as many variations of poker as there are days in the year. In no time I'm skilled in all the daredevil hands from four-card draw to deuces wild. Quinn also shows me tricks he learned from other soldiers—how to make a coin disappear, how to fold a paper swan.

One evening Aunt sets aside her needle and hoop and squeezes herself onto her piano stool to plunk out some songs. Aunt hasn't touched the piano since all three boys had been dispatched. She plays a few hymns, and then the strokes of her fingers on the keys choose Will's favorite song, "Lilly Dale." On purpose or by accident, I cannot say.

Tears spring to my eyes. The very walls and corners of the rooms seem to watch me. As Aunt lurches into the third verse, I slip from the room, resolving to come back and steal away the pages from

Aunt Clara's songbook. I don't want her to play it again. I want to go to the coat closet to be alone, but Quinn catches up with me in the foyer.

"Mother is a foolish, selfish old woman who sees nothing wrong with imposing her sentimental impulses," Quinn says, taking advantage of my stillness to move close and caress my cheek. "You mustn't let her come between us."

"It's more than that. Will haunts you, too," I say. "It's Will who is between us. Not Aunt."

"Only if you let him." His arm is encircling me, an antidote to the darkness all around us. His other hand leaves its touch on my cheek as he digs into his trousers' pocket. "Wear this," he says. "I found it in Aunt's jewelry box. But it's always been your ring, my dear Fleur. And so is the promise that goes with it."

"Oh." I am taken aback. "But…"

"Of course I plan to replace it with another—a ring that's meant for only us. But I just need a bit of time, until I begin to make my own money. Until then, you *must* have something. So that Mother— so that everyone—understands my intentions." Quinn's forehead is creased with worry. "But frankly, it's the promise that I am hoping for, from you. I want you to be my wife, Jennie. If you'll have me."

He slips the ring onto my finger. I blink at the twinkling stones, the garnets and diamond. I am speechless, anxiety stirring as my mind is seized with a memory of that long-ago holiday in Nantucket, the sudden crash of a wave over my head, the hard rush and slam of my body against the sand, the undertow dragging me back as I struggled to move forward to shore.

"Oh, yes," I say. "Of course, my love." My voice deliberately raised against my fears as I pull him close against me.

271. RHINOCEROS

It's hard to believe that this beast exists —
Would it be too difficult to photograph, I wonder?
Surely, it does not appear to be swift-moving

A spy hears Eurything and forgets NothinG

A SPY must Trust His Instinck

24.

O ne more chapter," I plead.

"Jennie, I can't. I'm hoarse."

There's a squeak of the leather chair when Uncle Henry heaves himself up to pour his last brandy. Quinn slaps the book cover shut on another chapter of *Barchester Towers*. And then the draining sip of cocoa on my tongue and Aunt's eggshell-thin cup clicks in its saucer. Mavis tiptoes in to take the tray.

After good-nights are said, Quinn and I confer our last thoughts and lingering embraces outside his door.

"Try to sleep tonight," he whispers. "You're not getting nearly the rest you need. I see it in your eyes."

"You worry too much. I'm fit as a fiddle," I assure him, and offer my mouth for one last brush against his lips. Though I am in dread of what awaits, I dare not confess it.

There is no use delaying the inevitable. I take my candle and tread the flights of stairs to my attic, where I slip into my nightgown, say my prayers, and burrow under my quilts. I don't blow out my candle.

It has been one week and one day since Quinn's and my engagement. Perhaps this night will be different. I hold on to that hope like a child's doll as I curl up, a snail without a shell, in dread wait of what lies just beyond sleep.

No sooner have my bones and mind relaxed into unconsciousness than I am slammed out of sleep by nameless, abject terror. I sit up in a sweat, thrashing, the scream dying in my throat as I struggle against the sensation of choking. I can almost feel Will's breath on my cheek, the pressure of his body on the bedclothes. "Stop! Stop! What do you want from me?"

The candle has guttered and the fire gone dead. Just as it has every night before.

My shaking fingers grope to find the matches. The jolt from darkness to flickering light reveals nothing more than my ordinary room. My twisted covers, hot cheeks, and pounding heart are the only evidence of disturbance.

I recite a simple prayer, which helps me find my breath again. Then I leave my bed to retrieve my scrapbook, where I turn to the page where I've affixed my locket. I can't bear to wear it anymore. I stare at Will's photograph for a long time. "Maybe you never loved me after all," I whisper to his image. "It's a truth I must face. You think I have betrayed you, William. But you have become a demon."

A tear slips down my cheek. Not once in his life or mine have I spoken unkindly toward Will. Even now it feels wrong. But it is harder and harder for me to recognize that carefree, high-spirited boy who went away to war and never came home.

Tonight the entire house is sleeping. Everyone but me. Slipping down the stairs, I pause by Quinn's shut door. No, better not disturb him with my wild tales of ghostly visitations. Creeping farther down the hall, I decide to visit Will's room.

It has been closed up for months, save Mavis's occasional perfunctory dusting, and when I enter, the trapped air holds a faint, stale odor of lye and must. The sickle moon casts a glow on every object, safe and familiar. My fingers drift over Will's bookshelves, his pigeonhole desk, and his velveteen hobbyhorse, McHale, which stands in a corner. Beneath sparse lashes the horse's glass eye fixes on me, almost as if to beckon me closer.

There is no anger here. I lie down on Will's four-poster bed, the dark core of the room, and immediately I'm enfolded by my past, where I am once again at Benjamin Hodge's birthday party. An October afternoon of Brookline friends and amusements, and after lunch we'd played Sardines, a game that required one person to hide and the rest of us to find and then hide with him—until one last, lone searcher remained.

Will had been picked as "It," and I'd found him almost immediately in the Hodges' barn, wedged in the back of a hay bale. I'd tucked in next to him, and we'd nearly laughed ourselves sick listening to the others scurry through the door and then decide against making the climb to where we'd buried ourselves away, our arms wound around each other's waists. Not yet sweet on each other, but alert with possibilities we could not have yet articulated.

It is only when I hear Mavis's knock and her exclamation, "For the love of heaven, here you are!" that I am awake again.

It is morning. Astoundingly, I have slept through the entire night.

"We've been up for hours looking for you!" says Mavis.

"I don't...I didn't..." I yawn and stretch. What a wonderful rest.

"Hurry, now. I've got a fresh dress right here. You'll need to change quick to catch the last of breakfast. You've had us in a tizzy.

Missus Sullivan was just about ready to declare you a slattern who'd eloped with some fancy man from the city."

"How unsurprising." I am yanking out of my nightgown and then splashing with water from the pitcher and basin that Mavis has brought. When I enter the dining room for breakfast, it's with a sense that my strange antics have been recently discussed.

"Jennie, it has come to my attention that you must move into the yellow room," Aunt announces first thing.

I blink across at her. "The yellow room? Are you quite sure?"

"Do you propose sleeping again in Will's room as you did last night? Do you find that an appropriate arrangement?"

Chastened, I look down at my plate.

"A perfect choice," Quinn adds, so swiftly that I realize it was his idea. "After all, *I'm* not moving. I'm jolly as a bear in your old room, with my books and papers taking up every shelf and crevice."

Uncle Henry rustles his newspaper but doesn't rub at his head.

"Thank you, Aunt Clara." It might be the first time in months I've said these words to Aunt and meant them. Outwardly the yellow room holds more worth than the ring on my finger. It is a room fit for the lady of the house.

Which, apparently, is what I am again.

"The yellow room's the prettiest, I've always thought," Quinn murmurs when he finds me there later that afternoon. My unpacking has been distracted by the discovery of a book of zoological prints. "I hope you do, too. And won't feel compelled to wander."

I stiffen. "Quinn, I didn't mean to fall asleep in Will's room. But late at night, I am plagued…"

"Yes, yes. I know." His eyes flicker. "You're not the only one with ghosts."

On the end table Lotty has left a tray with a fresh pot of tea to stave off the chill of the day. I prepare Quinn a cup, which he takes as he moves to the window, twitching the drape.

"Oh!" The book falls from my lap as I see it. My heart is pounding. I didn't realize that this was my view. Through the frost on the glass, I can see the outline of the butternut tree.

"What? It's only our swinging tree," says Quinn.

"It's the…shape. It has always reminded me of a witch." I attempt a laugh, though the sight of the tree truly scares me.

Quinn frowns. "I'll have the hired man chop it down. We'll plant some weeping cherries there. Come next spring, you'll have a view of pink blossoms instead of that crooked old crone." He turns from the window to retrieve and hand back the book that has tumbled across the carpet. "What's this you're reading?"

"*Animals of the Orient.*" I shuffle through, looking for the page. "If I saw a rhinoceros, if there really is such a beast, I'd faint dead away. There, look." I find it, with its terrifying one-horned head and splayed feet.

"Let's travel to the Orient this fall."

"Trot the globe together, you and I?" I ask softly.

"Why not? Lately I feel as if anything's possible with you at my side." As Quinn moves to pull me up to face him, my lips spontaneously nip the bottom of his chin, grazing it. Quinn's mouth isn't as full as Will's, nor as yielding, but his need is imperative, with rougher edges. It excites me.

Did I desire Quinn even then? Is that why I am haunted by the anger of his brother?

The sound of a polite cough makes me jump.

"Madame Broussard." I step away from Quinn. "I didn't know you were expected here."

"Your aunt summoned me." The dressmaker looks embarrassed. She smooths her impeccably smooth shirtwaist. "I've just done another round of fittings for Mrs. Pritchett. She sent me to find you. She told me you'll need a new dress for young Mr. Pritchett's dinner party."

"Dinner party?" I'm confused.

"My twentieth birthday," Quinn explains. "Mother wants a lavish spectacle. There's no getting her off it."

"But we hardly—"

"It's an occasion. We can announce our engagement then, so you'll need to look as sweet as a tea rose."

"A new party dress is such a luxury in these times."

Quinn's fingers fan off my words. "What's sauce for the goose— why, I'm forever dashing into town to the tailor for this and that." He taps his heels. "If I'm going to play the dandy on my birthday, there's got to be enough in the coffers for a frock for you."

"I haven't clipped out a pattern in ages," I protest. "I have no idea what's in fashion."

"I'll bring patterns next time," Madame assures. "But with your flair, Mademoiselle, you ought to sew the lacework yourself."

But after she leaves, I speak my mind. "Quinn, for heaven's sake. The whole house has overheard your epic battles with Aunt about the budget," I remind him. "I could wear a flour sack to your party and have fun."

"*Our* party. And perish all thoughts of flour sacks. You forget, Father has agreed that I should start my clerkship at the bank next month."

"You feel well enough to work?"

"I've got the strength of a thousand men since we've been betrothed." Quinn winds me to him, kissing me again. I feel the warm print of his lips burnishing mine. I lean into the crook of his elbow, but when I look up again, I see it.

Traced as if by a finger into the fogged window glass, the image of the crooked little heart nearly stops my own. I break from Quinn's embrace, my insides lurching, my knuckles stifling my scream.

"Is this your wretched idea of a joke?"

"What…?" He crosses to the window to inspect. "Why, it's just like the heart on the butternut tree."

"Why did you do that? Why?" My voice saws upward in panic.

"Me? This is ridiculous." Quinn erases the heart in one wipe of his shirtsleeve. "Jennie, I don't want to play this game. We both know you drew on the glass."

"*I* did? How outrageous!"

"Is it? Because it's just the sort of thing you *would* do," Quinn continues. "Spiritualist nonsense. Your way of introducing this exact conversation."

"That's a terrible thing to accuse! I hope you don't mean it. Especially when we never speak of the others."

"I do mean it. And please, speak of your brother and mine all you wish, but your actions—your midnight wanderings, your tumble into Will's bed—are quite on point. I worry, Jennie, of course I do. I live in terror that your grief might suffocate our future. Ever since our engagement, you've hardly slept—"

"That's not my fault, I—"

"—and you're as thin as a rake, and the tired rings under your eyes—"

"—So now you think I'm a ghoul!"

"You know I think you're lovely, Fleur, but you're not in your best health."

191

"Quinn, I didn't draw on the glass."

He takes another step away from me. "Who, then? My brother's damaged and wandering spirit? As a reminder of his everlasting love for you?" I feel his exasperation pulse through every moment. I have no answer, save the tears that well in my eyes.

"If this is your game, then so be it," he says levelly. "But remember, love isn't a nightmare, or an empty bed, or a print on fogged glass. Love is flesh and blood. Don't you see me? Because I'm right here, and I'm very much yours."

Then he leaves, shutting the door firmly behind him. I'm pained to have led the conversation into such a fraught and stupid place. Now I'm alone with my view and a knowledge that no matter how lovely this room is, it won't give me the peace I crave.

I press my forehead to the window.

"If I'm a ghoul, Will, it's your doing," I say under my breath. "Let me have my future. If you ever loved me, you'd free me."

Of course, no answer.

Later, on my way to find Quinn and smooth his ruffled feathers, I pass the front coat closet. Curiosity shifts in me; I can't resist.

A spy must trust his instinct.

I press my ear to the door. Nothing. But then I grip the knob and turn it. My wary eyes scan the shadowed winter cloaks and wraps. Everything is just as it should be.

I slip inside, closing the door behind me, and sit as I used to, with held breath and squeezed limbs. I shut my eyes the way Toby did. "I find my best thoughts in this closet," Toby had said. As if his thoughts were loose, ripe apples he'd collected and hidden here.

Sparks and stars float across my closed eyes. Sightless, I can almost feel my twin again. The darkness is alive and intelligent, and I fancy that I catch a bit of Toby's own boyish scent, grass and cotton. I'm not sure how long I am burrowed there. My hand crawls to find a jam pot from our stockpile. My mouth is suddenly flooded with the taste of strawberries from sweeter and happier days. I drift...

I'm startled from my reverie by voices in the corridor outside.

"Tut, tut—I've been looking for you, Mr. Pritchett," Aunt Clara exclaims. "You need to write that check to Gladwell's so that I may place my order. We are much in debt there."

"Don't see why we need new wallpaper when the old hasn't fallen down on us yet." But Uncle Henry's voice sounds enfeebled as always when bending to Aunt. "And this talk of debt is a tax on my health."

"You've never concerned yourself about our debt before, husband. There's no need to start now." Aunt's voice is deceptively sweet. "Anyway, it's a passing vexation until Quinn pays off everything as he'd promised and sets us right as rain."

Uncle Henry answers in a mumble, and he and Aunt part on a sour note as he storms off while Aunt patters away in the opposite direction.

Alone again, I wait a few more minutes so that nobody catches me darting out of the closet.

A spy hears everything and forgets nothing.

I had no idea Aunt relied so heavily on Quinn's future earnings. And yet she continues to spend with foolish abandon—why do we need new wallpaper? I'll have to report on these silly extravagances that continue to flow from Aunt Clara's whims and Uncle Henry's henpecked pen.

A debt to Gladwell's is news to me, too. Costs must be piling up. This private information is useful. Was it only chance that has drawn me to this closet? On impulse, I spin on my heel and return to the door. I place my hand on the knob and pull. But now the door won't budge.

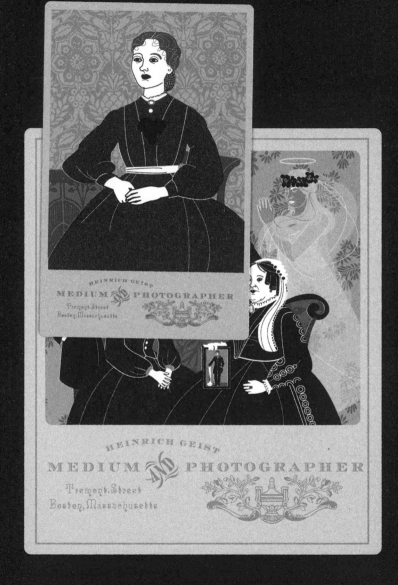

HEINRICH GEIST

MEDIUM AND PHOTOGRAPHER

Tremont Street
Boston, Massachusetts

HEINRICH GEIST

MEDIUM AND PHOTOGRAPHER

Tremont Street
Boston, Massachusetts

A Spy Must RetanE
at Least One Loyal Ally-Ance.

Flora Wortley

Rosemary Wortley

If everyone knew
how much Flora
gossips and Rosemary
eats, they mightn't be
so quick to accept a
calling card from either
Sister.

25.

Don't you see? Will can't let me go." I slide both prints, side by side, in front of Geist. "Sometimes I think he wants to drive me completely mad."

The flicker in the photographer's eye mortifies me. He must find me ridiculous, but I refuse to buckle. It took some conniving for me to slip into the city today on the pretext of a visit to Madame Broussard. Now that I'm here, I've made a pact with myself not to leave Geist's house without his promise of help.

"But don't *you* see, Miss Lovell? Any human hand could have—"

"I didn't ink either photo. I swear it."

Geist heaves up from his chair and folds his spectacles, slipping them into his breast pocket. "What do you want me to do?"

"Mr. Geist, you're my only chance to free myself of Will. You yourself told me that photography can be a portal."

"My child, we took your photograph. By your account, your sleuthing was successful. For you *say*"—and now I detect the brushstrokes of impatience in Geist's voice—"that the heart inked onto your print led you to your locket, and then to one brother admitting that the other had been hanged in dishonor. You *say* Will's spirit wanted your forgiveness, and that you granted it." He steeples his fingers. "Your fiancé—*former* fiancé—is seven months dead. You *say* you've accepted that, too. What more is there to communicate?"

Under Geist's eye, I stand poker-straight while keeping my eyes and voice true. "I'd accept everything if I felt at peace with it. But I don't. Mr. Geist, every night, save one, I've awakened to feel a noose around my neck. Just as it might have tightened around his. I feel his rage." Now I speak out loud my gnawing fears. "I think Will wants me to come to him. I think he's trying to send me to the edge. And possibly beyond."

Geist cocks his head. "Why would he do that?"

"Perhaps because if he can't have me, then he doesn't want anyone else to have me?" I'm embarrassed to speak of such intimate matters, and my composure is melting quicker than ice on a skillet. "I don't even know what I expect you to do for me. It's not as if you can offer Will's soul for me to study like Turkish tea leaves." My voice dips. "But something is very wrong, and I am sure that I'll have no peace until I make it right."

Certainly my sniffling hasn't impressed either of us, but Geist lets me carry on for a bit before he steers me gently by my elbow from his sitting room to the foyer.

"Miss Lovell, look to your own heart," he says as he wraps me in my cloak. "You might find that some of your agitation is self-inflicted."

"Self-inflicted?" My throat scrapes the word in my throat. The exhaustion of all my sleepless nights hits me like a wave. "But I'm wrecked."

"Yet I see you're again betrothed, yes?"

"To Quinn, yes." Under his hawkish eye, I fumble. "We've always been close."

"You're blushing."

"No."

"I'm not sitting in judgment of you, my dear. Merely observing. But let me offer this—it's natural to feel some guilt and uncertainty. You loved one brother, and now you love the other. Your heart might need time to catch up." Geist takes my left hand in his, tapping the fourth finger where my engagement ring sparkles again. I flush. I'm not sure how to defend myself, or if I even need to, when he changes subjects. "Young Pritchett came to visit me last week."

"Quinn did? Why?"

"He wanted to purchase the original photograph I took of your family. He said that he wanted to destroy it. Spiritualist bunk, et cetera. He made no bones about his mistrust of my profession."

"Quinn thinks I suffer from delusions. And, yes, we have different opinions about your craft. Surely Quinn isn't your first skeptic."

"Quite so. Nor will he be my last."

"I apologize if he was curt."

In Geist's face I sense an apology reluctantly accepted. "Miss Lovell, I don't mean to hurry you off, but I have a busy schedule today." He raises his voice. "Viviette!"

As Mavis whisks around from the pantry—now that I'm a lady again, I'm not allowed to travel unaccompanied—a visibly pregnant Viviette hastens down the stairs.

Geist takes his leave as Viviette helps us with our bonnets and gloves. Opening the front door, she levels me in her anthracite gaze.

"That first time," she hisses, her breath so close that my nostrils detect an odor of pickled herring, "when you all was here, I was visited, too, I was. An evil presence come into that room with you and your kin. Evil as evil is."

"Stop it, Viviette. You're just trying to scare me," I tell her. "Though I don't know why…"

She webs her bony fingers over her belly, guarding it. "I told my fright to Mister Geist, and next thing I did was leave this place at once. I feared the curse might be catched onto my unborn."

"You talk of catching a curse as if it's a pox," I rebuke.

"I know what I know." Viviette yanks up her chin as she bumps the side of her thumb repeatedly against her breastbone. "I got the sight. Nobody would deny it. When there's a demon close, it infects me. When that same demon returns, it strikes me exactly the same."

Surely *I* am not a demon in her eyes. What have I ever done to her? Why would she accuse me? My fingers fuss with my bonnet ribbon. "Viviette, I'll thank you to keep your low opinion of me—and my family—to yourself."

"An evil business you're tangled in," she continues doggedly. "It's a shame you're too close to see it proper."

"Good day," I manage, though I can't mask that she's shocked me.

Out on the street, my heart beats hard as a hammer even as I shrug it off. "Silly chit." I sniff at Mavis. "I'd wager the most demonic thing Viviette has encountered lately is her own sour-pickle breath."

"Miss High 'n' Mighty's been posing as an angel too long," Mavis agrees. "And a fine one she'd make these days, in her condition. Did you finish your business with Mister Geist?"

"No, but he's finished with me," I admit. "He thinks I'm full of nonsense."

Mavis allows a pause. "If it's any comfort, it's not just you, Miss

Jennie, who feels a…restlessness in Pritchett House. We talk about it sometimes, downstairs."

Her declaration surprises me. I thought that my haunting was for me alone.

"Tell me what you mean, Mavis."

She bites her lip. "Oh, it's wee things, here and there. Like from the fairy stories my mum used to tell us. I can't help but notice the drafts that get into a room. A fire blown out. A window pushed open on a cold day. A shadow flung 'cross a carpet, but not a body attached to it. And there's been times, Miss, when I'll look up from my dusting or making up a bed, and I know clear as church bells that I'm being watched by someone, or something." Her eyes meet mine. "There's talk that Mister Will got corrupted in the war. That he turned bad. Have y'ever thought, Miss, that it might be best *not* to try and make peace with his spirit?"

I am at a loss. "But what else is there? If not peace and forgiveness?"

"I agree to a point, Miss. But if there's a demon, why, you've got to drive him out." Her fist smacks her palm. "Before he is the unholy death of you. For there are ways." I sense these thoughts have been thickening in Mavis's head awhile, as she recites them. "A Bible in the windowsill should help. Or hang a crucifix. Or get a cat. A good Maine coon cat'll shoo the devil from a house better than most people. P'raps you could ask Father Sheehan to come sprinkle every room with holy water."

Her solutions are childish, but her emotions are fervent. I wonder how far and wide these tales of Pritchett House have spread.

The wind nearly blows us backward once we turn the corner onto Federal Street, where I'm greeted in the bank's atrium by the spectacle of both Wortley sisters, overdressed in flourishes and furbelows. They are both on me at once.

"Jennie, what luck!" trills Flora.

"We were just having our spring hats trimmed at Mrs. Hawksby's, and then we stepped in here to wait for our carriage!"

"Do tell us when we can call on you, Jennie, for we hear such delightful news—"

"Mama wrote all about your turn of fortune when we were in Concord visiting Aunt Sal last week. Didn't you land feet-up in the butter! So Quinn isn't gone mad, as most everyone thought. He'll be working right here in this bank, and you'll be the new Mrs. Pritchett. When Flora read the note, she nearly dropped out of her chair with envy! She's been in love with Quincy Pritchett since she was in bloomers."

"Hush, Rosemary, I am not—but show us your ring!"

"Yes, let's see!" Rosemary captures my hand, then flinches as her voice drops. "Why, my dear, that's the very same, the diamond and garnets—"

Flora gapes. "Nooo...not *Will*'s ring!"

"The one your aunt yanked off—"

"Aunt Clara specially wanted me to have it back," I fib, though I could curse the flush blooming in my face. "It's a family piece, after all."

"Certainly it would be a waste of an adequate stone." Flora smirks, and I know she is burning to spread the gossip of my twice-used ring.

"Are you planning a big June wedding?" Rosemary asks. "Think of us, dear heart, when you're choosing bridesmaids. Whatever you do, don't make me wear chartreuse, for it drains all the color from my face. Peach or mint would do nicely, though."

"Oooh, that reminds me—will you serve ice cream?" Flora clasps her hands.

Rosemary giggles. "Flora, you'll eat yourself to death before you find a husband!"

"Sister, you are too droll!" Flora grates a laugh, as she jabs Rosemary hard in the ribs. "There's Mr. Jake now, waving for us. Here, take my card. I just had them done in the very latest design. And do you have one for me? No? Never mind, then. Good-bye, Jennie, darling." They exit the bank in a babble.

"*Jennie, darling!* Did you hear that?" I turn to Mavis. "Everyone knows that family's the worst kind of snobs. It was only two months ago they all but refused my friendship."

"Oh, but Miss, this wedding'll make you the belle of Brookline." Mavis chuckles. "*Both* those sisters had set their caps tight for Mister Quinn 'fore he left for the war. My sister, Betsey, howled to watch 'em fuss and preen."

I smile. "I'd forgotten."

Mavis twinkles. "He was always tweaking one sister off t'other. And never serious with neither. Oh, no man in his right mind would marry either of those two spoiled nobodies!"

But I'm not thinking of the plight of the charmless Wortley sisters. The echoes of too many voices hold my ear.

Didn't you land feet-up in the butter...

Isn't gone mad, as most everyone thought...

A demon close. A bad business.

Quinn will only laugh it off and tell me that it's the rare soul who's truly happy for another's good fortune. Especially not a fraudulent medium, or a family of social climbers, or a pregnant servant girl.

Still, I cringe from public speculation, so easily given and so bruising. I make up my mind to order some engraved calling cards just as soon as Quinn and I are wed.

"A June wedding would be beautiful," I mention to Mavis on the ride back, quietly enough that Uncle Henry doesn't hear. "But I'd prefer something modest. Anything extravagant might be dishonorable to Will's memory."

Mavis pulls on her agreeable face, though I know she thinks I ought to do just as I please and have as sumptuous a wedding as I want. Honor be damned.

I have to wonder if Will would have paid me the same courtesy.

PRITCHETT HOUSE

Mr. and Mrs. Henry Pritchett
request the pleasure of your company
at a Birthday Dinner
in honor of their son

Quincy Emory Pritchett

Friday, the Twenty-eigth of February
at Seven o'Clock in the Evening;

Dancing to follow.

Winthrop Road
Brookline, Massachusetts

An invitation that didn't pass muster.

26.

On the afternoon of the party, the house is hushed. Expectant. It's a change. All week, until this morning, it churned with activity. But now the florists and confectioners have gone, dropping off their arrangements, their bowls of trailing ivy and hothouse roses, their iced petits fours, their candied lavender and orange-blossom petals, and other delicacies beyond the household's practical expertise.

Though our humble kitchen has been busy, too. The lobster bisque, the dripping, spit-roasted beef, the waft of potatoes broiled in tarragon and butter have been planned, prepared, and executed under Mrs. Sullivan's scrupulous eye. She has chosen most of her recipes from before the war, and I can't help but worry that they are too extravagant for the sober climate. Certainly they are tastes that I have not sampled in years. The aroma alone sets my stomach into embarrassing gurgles of anticipation.

The table is set with the best lace and linens. Every stick of silver has been polished to luster. Passing through the dining room earlier, I imagine that the very walls and windows hold their breath, as if nothing less than a coronation is taking place tonight.

Quinn calls this evening his mother's folly, but he'd never trust

Aunt Clara to make it a success, so he himself has paid personal attention to every detail. From the wording on Aunt Clara's carefully penned invitations to the order of the dancing—and the proper moment, just before the port and cheese, for announcing our engagement.

Such a delicate evening couldn't be left to Aunt. We're both well aware that our news must be managed with grace. "And with respect for our dear brothers, William and Tobias. They are our very own guardian angels, and we pray that they will guide us with temperance and protect us from life's unhappy vagaries," Quinn had recited late last night as we'd sat together, watching the dying embers in the sitting room. Quinn had wanted to practice some of his speech out loud to me before he faced down Brookline society.

"Yes, quite right," I'd answered.

"Then, what's wrong?"

"I suppose I'm fearful that people might judge me harshly," I admitted. "One brother, now the other. Geist said my heart might not have caught up to—"

"Ah, to hell with whatever Geist says." Quinn's brows had knit as he'd folded the paper into his pocket. "He's a moldering old bachelor and a gypsy swindler to boot. You know that many wartime widows are remarrying, Jennie. People aren't meant to live lonely." But then he'd turned boyish and clinging, dropping from his chair to rest his head in my lap. My hand had reached to stroke the ginger curls, soft as a child's. I am taken aback. Quinn was so rarely given to acts of vulnerability. I think of how Will used to waggle and bounce, throwing himself at me like an excited puppy.

"You are right, of course," I'd whispered.

"We've been far too isolated here, haven't we?" he'd whispered back. "It's bound to make us worry over how we'll conduct ourselves in society. But a reintroduction to our friends and neighbors ought to do everyone some good. I'll mourn both our brothers for the rest of my life, but let us resolve to shine some light in each other's lives as well."

"You're right, dear Quinn. Let's."

How I'd wanted to put my faith in this thought, how dismayed I'd been that its comfort doesn't hold.

That night, as I'd lain awake, I'd made a secret prayer that this party will be the prelude to a farewell. Of one thing I was certain: for as long as I remain at Pritchett House, I will live in anxiety and dread.

When the time is right I'll suggest to Quinn what has weighed heavy on my mind—that we need to move from here. We can live in Boston or Hartford, away from Aunt and Uncle. Away from this house of nightmares. No Bible, no prayers or blessing by Father Shechan or Reverend Meeks could possibly drive out the vengeful spirit in the house. We will escape it instead. I want Mavis to come with me, too, though I haven't dared put the question to her yet. Pritchett House is all she knows. For now I will keep my plan secret.

That night and the next day pass uneasily as I help Aunt Clara with the minute arrangements of seating charts and music selection.

"Do you think everybody will come?" I ask.

Patches of angry pink appear in Aunt's cheeks. "Are you implying that anyone would dare refuse?" she snaps. "Jennie, we are *Pritchetts*."

Not I, not really, not yet. But I use her dudgeon to take quick leave, retreating to my room, where I wait for Madame Broussard, who will be making Aunt's and my last-minute alterations.

Sunlight has ignited my bedroom, but the room itself is cold—just as it had been in my attic. I build up the fire and settle back with some lacework.

Percy, the calico kitten that Mavis has given me in secret, looks up at me from his basket. So far, the kitten has not seemed the least bit troubled by malevolent spirits. In fact, he seems quite content with his flannel-lined bed and yarn mouse. He is a sweet thing with unblinking amber eyes, and what Aunt doesn't know of his presence won't hurt her.

The kitten's belled collar tinkles faintly as he jumps into my lap. His purring is warmth and music. My eyes close into memories of a long-ago sled ride. I am waiting my turn on the top of a hill as Quinn prepares to launch Will and me. Quinn had pushed hard and fast, and the sled's bells jingled as we'd whooped—our delight turning almost instantly to terror as one runner caught a buried rock and sent us jettisoning into the air, flipping over the sled, slamming our bodies through space to land hard and skid against the ice-packed earth.

"You did it on purpose!" Will had accused his brother in a spitting fury as we'd collected ourselves. "You wanted to scare everyone off the sled—why, you probably planted the rock, too—and I'm gonna tan your arse for it!" Invoking the stable boy's rough language and tone so aptly, it shocked us all.

"Toby, stop him!" I called through my drenched, mittened hands as Toby chased Will, who was chasing Quinn up and down the meadow. Afterward we'd all trod back into the house for cider and molasses cake. The chaos of the event soon forgotten as we'd all indulged our sweet tooth. Later Quinn admitted to us all that he'd wanted to see what would happen if he pushed us with all his strength—"but I didn't hide the rock, Will. And I can't apologize for something I didn't do."

Yet Will had refused to accept this, looking daggers at his brother for the rest of the day.

"*Mon dieu!*" I wake with Madame's eyes on me. "This room is freezing! How do you sleep in such condition? But we must hurry, it's nearly four."

"Oh…" I wince. Strangely, I feel bruised all over, a phantom pain as if I'd taken that fall from the sled only minutes ago. I glance at the mantel clock, and I see with shock that it is stopped at half past two.

The undertow, catching back my past, drowning me deep inside it.

The room is like ice. The fire has died and the window is frosted. Percy has left my lap to shiver in a ball in his basket.

"Let me light the fire. *Il fait si froid ici* than outdoors, but I am not sure how that could be."

Outside, the afternoon sun is a butterscotch blaze, sinking fast and igniting the outline of the tree.

"*Alors*, we have one last fitting," says Madame. "I pray you have not lost more weight."

She will be disappointed. I take my position, standing on the ottoman in my whalebone corset as Madame unwraps the bottle-green silk dress along with its pounds of accompanying petticoats plus metal-hooped crinoline.

"These latest French fashions are the tiniest bit scandalous, especially with that neckline dipping ever so slightly off your shoulders," Madame murmurs. "You will be the talk of the soiree." She sinks to her hands and knees, the better to make last-minute adjustments to the point-jupe cords that pick up my skirt.

"So heavy. I feel as if I've doubled my weight," I remark.

"Eh, I wish." Madame pinches some of the dress fabric, loose at the waist, though she's taken it in once before. She works in silence, saving her thoughts until she finishes. "You're a sparrow in peacock finery," she pronounces lightly, but there's truth in the joke. My collarbone juts, my eyes are hollowed, even my hair lacks the luster for my upsweep. Like the rest of me, it seems to wilt, and when I slap at my cheeks they look as garish red as gypsy kisses in my wan face.

I drop my eyes to the dressmaker, who is knotting her needle. "I'm sorry that you won't be staying on for dinner, Madame."

"*Non, non*—I'm not one for crowds." She stands, gathering her spools and needles into her sewing basket. "But I'd advise you to test your shoes, Mademoiselle," she says, as we both glance over at them. Ivory kid leather in a pouched silk box. "Two inches off the ground will alter your perspective. You must learn to walk before you can waltz in them."

"Quite right." I jump down from the ottoman, and Madame assists with the shoehorn and binds the straps then sends me tottering down the corridor. I wobble up and down the flight of stairs. At the end of the hall, I try a curtsy, then brave a dip and twirl. Madame applauds.

"*À bientôt*," she says as she kisses each of my cheeks. "Young Mr. Pritchett desires me to return next week to plan your wedding trousseau."

"Thank you, Madame." My heart lifts. A trousseau. I've imagined mine since I was a young girl. The trunk trays of delicate undergarments, the nightcaps and linens, the yards of laces, the variety of fabrics—pongee and pique, silk and velvet and Swiss muslin. For a moment I am almost envious of Madame, who presides over the arrangements of so many trousseaux while a bride must settle on only one. But now I will heed her advice and learn to walk in these ridiculous shoes so that tonight I might be a gazelle on Quinn's arm.

Lemon-oil polish holds a strong scent of expectation. Everything has been aired out, sudsed over, or plumped up for the party, even rooms where no guest will tip a toe inside. I pause on the landing to stare out the window, where Madame's trap waits. Soon this view will be filled with carriages. A rare spectacle. Toby loved dinner parties, though he could be mischievous. So many voices to eavesdrop in on. So many secrets to absorb.

A spy must never let down his guard.

Pritchett House is a theater before the curtain rises, with the principal actors offstage. Aunt and Uncle are in their respective rooms, dressing and presumably bickering, while Quinn has rushed off in the carriage to the newspaper offices to personally submit the announcement of our engagement.

"The most precious errand of my day," he'd spoken in my ear, sending sparks up my spine.

Servants pass me with quick deferential bows. Some unfamiliar faces have been hired on for just this evening.

As I try my heels on the next flight of stairs, I run into Mavis. Her arms are weighted with the tea tray. "Why, you're a picture, Miss," she breathes. She herself looks exhausted and can hardly perk up a smile or wait for my response before she disappears into Aunt's lair.

At the end of the hall I pause at the entrance to Uncle Henry's study. Though this is his private sanctuary, I dare myself to enter. After all, no room should feel off-limits to me. Not as the future Mrs. Pritchett.

Defiant, I brace myself. I open the door and loop the room, one

QUINCY EMORY PRITCHETT

February 20, 1865

Dear Father,

Pursuant to your request of last week, here is my Stated
Letter of Intention. First, I would respectfully ask for a
formal Interview with Federal Bank for a possible
Position... ...thermore, I
...matters

Dearest Jennie,

I write on this Floor of packed Earth, with little Light,
my Hands scratched by Brambles and Blood beneath my ...
and looking through my Bandages. Oftentimes these Days ...
if I chanced to see you on the Street, would you even recognize me? For
I hardly know my Own Reflection. Once I Struck a Man with my
Bayonet so that his Blood Splattered hot over my Face. He looked me
Square in the Eyes as he fell, and I did not flinch and ~~~~~
~~~~~ this was my True Self

to be taken Prisoner, which may indeed be

though we may never again meet on Earth,
you to know that I always meant
I do want
not find Trouble, there are many of us in Harm's way
one broken Neck they say will be an example to others ~~~~
and I know not how to make this Confession
but to write the Truth of my Love ~~~~~~~
~~~~~ with Hope that you might think him a little. Jamie

For I am always thinking of you

J.M. WHITTEMORE & CO., 114 WASHINGTON ST., Boston

pinched step at a time. The room carries a whiff of authority, of old scotch and pipe tobacco and leather-bound books, and of Uncle's own pine-scented cologne. I am drawn to the clutter on Uncle's desk. Perhaps there is an opened ledger where I can see for myself what sort of expenses have been incurred this month.

The morning newspaper partially obscures the letter. But I recognize the handwriting. I pick it up.

It's a formal request for a meeting at the bank and for an explanation of the details of his trust. Quinn had told me he'd be composing just such a note to Uncle Henry. The contents aren't what I see. There are no magic words here.

My chemise has gone damp with sweat. Phrases stab my eyes; I snatch the paper, balling it so tight that my fingernails bite my palm. I am stuck and bleeding with the knowledge. It can't be undone. I back out of the study and run, my heels catching and digging into the carpet. On the landing I nearly sprain my ankle as I rush into my room, locking the door behind me.

"Please, dear Lord. It's not true. Don't let it be true."

Will's last letter from Camp Sumter is kept with his others safe inside the pages of my scrapbook. So many times I'd knelt before the hearth or grate, intending to destroy it. To torch its physical reminder. Turn it to ash. At the last minute, I never could. It was Will's final clutch of contact with me before I'd lost him altogether. Or so I'd thought.

Steeling myself, I unfold it. Then I smooth out Quinn's note to Uncle Henry and place it next to Will's prison confession.

The blocks of paragraph, the cutting strokes of his uppercase letters, the back slant of his lower loops. My finger traces these same words as my lips repeat them, hearing their fierce braggadocio. I'd never found Will's identity in that final letter. His words had never imprinted as the young man I could claim as my own. So I clung to the assertion that he'd changed from the war. How could he not have been changed?

I'd read that letter with my own pain surging through me. I'd read that confession with hardly a thought to the writer. For it hadn't struck me, not once, that it wasn't the same man at all.

Right-handed, Quinn's letters had been elegant as a woman's. In readapting to his left hand, his style has taken on some of his brother's traits. The narrow loops, that blown-back slant. Some of Will, but much of Quinn remains on the page.

With shaking hands, I tuck both letters into my skirt pocket and hurry from my bedroom. Wheeling around the staircase and gripping the banister for balance, I see Madame in her cloak at the mirror, making fastidious adjustments to her hat as she prepares to leave.

"Madame," I whisper. But new doubts strangle my breath.

Here it is, laid out in front of me. The sense of what I ought to have seen all along. And yet, staring into the horror of the moment, I'm numb. I need to force myself to action, but I am paralyzed by what that means for me.

A monster. He is a monster.

A cry escapes my lips. Startled, Madame looks up and catches my eye in the mirror's reflection. "Why, Mademoiselle Jennie, what is it? What has happened?"

I want to hide, but instead I run, hurtling down the stairs to grasp hold of the dressmaker's wrists, my eyes beseeching her. "Take me away from here, Madame. Please, I must go at once!"

JULY 10 1864

SO-CALLED "CURTIS'S RAIDERS" IN THE PRISON AT CAMP SUMTER AWAITING EXECUT
SKETCHED BY AN ENGLISH ARTIST.—[SEE PAGE 17.]

27.

In the mirror, the right hand becomes the left. In everything I saw, I now find its reflection. A young man looks into the mirror and another looks through. In replacing one brother with the other, the lock of the mystery comes unclasped. Now I smooth out the chain of the narrative, link by link.

A spy is foremost a code breaker.

Two brothers went to war. The older was a natural soldier, an optimist, and an athlete. Adored by everyone, invincible in his confidence. The younger brother was reserved, an acid wit with a taste for gambling and fine clothes. He stood in disdain of the elder's good and trusting nature while secretly craving all that his big brother had. Sometimes to the point where he pretended he had those things, too.

Away from home the younger brother befriended a soldier, another rogue like himself, who became a happy substitute when his blood brother loomed too disapproving or expected too much. Together, Quinn Pritchett and Nate Dearborn played cards, rolled dice, drank whiskey, and invented stories of their sweethearts back home—Franny Paddle and Jennie Lovell. The fact that Franny didn't exist, or that I was engaged to Will, didn't matter to these brothers-in-arms. The battlefield was not reality.

The friends honed their talent for gambling and then, inured by the monstrous horrors of the Wilderness, for grave robbing—*what use has a dead man for a watch or a ring or a pair of thick boots...*Thieving from corpses of fallen soldiers meant a wealth of treasures to barter, and others must have known of their cache. Rounded up with their company and forced into Camp Sumter, they would be naturally attracted to a gang of thieves, and the thieves to them. Charles Curtis, the leader of such a gang, knew how to put these young men's talents to good use—for a time. *We picked the adventure knowing there'd be no end but a bloody one...This was my true self.*

I can't complete the entire shape of this chain. It is not laid out flat in front of my eyes. What was Will's role in all this? Why did *he* end up a thief and Raider? What specific crime had he committed that he was delivered to the gallows at Camp Sumter? Why couldn't he have escaped with Quinn?

Madame had asked nothing of me when I'd asked her to take me away and given her Geist's address. I suppose the fear in my eyes had been enough. She'd simply tossed my cloak over my shoulders and hurried me out the front door to her coach. We hadn't spoken a word on the trip into Boston, though I'm sure her questions burned in her head.

My own mind is surprisingly lucid. I think of Viviette's baleful gaze on me all over again. I'd been mistaken. Viviette hadn't called me the demon; she had warned me of the demon. And Quinn's second visit had confirmed her suspicions.

"I'll wait for you." Madame finally breaks her silence as the carriage turns down the modest rectilinear block to stop in front of Geist's townhouse.

"No need. Mr. Geist will bring me home in his carriage," I dissuade her. "Truly, I'll be fine."

Madame looks doubtful, but my feet are brisk as I disembark. I wave her driver on. "Thank you, Madame."

Through the carriage window she watches me, but doesn't protest as the driver snaps the reins. Once she is departed and I've tripped up the steps to Geist's door, I'm faced with a dread sensation. Inside, darkness. Nobody is home.

With a sinking heart, I rap the brass knocker.

"You won't find him."

I whip around. The next-door housekeeper lists over the rail, as bloated as a bee. Tipsy I'd wager, and she has stepped outside for a few bracing moments of winter twilight before ducking back into her kitchen prison.

"Where did he go?"

She raises her hand with her slurred proclamation. "He did the right thing by her. With a ring on her finger, she can hold her head up."

I'm confused. "Who?"

"Him and her. The master and his maid. Run off together."

"You mean Mr. Geist and Viviette were...married?"

"Yes, Miss, in city hall, the day 'fore yesterday."

There's no way to hide my incredulity. "Where are they now?"

"On holiday. Took a train all the way up to Nova Scotia. Where no doubt they'll be up to their usual dev'lish monkeyshines. Developing those ghosty pitchers and plund'ring the souls of the dead." She genuflects.

My bewilderment must show on my face, for the housekeeper guffaws. "No, no, no. There's no romance there, Miss, lest you count the love of money. Everyone knows it was that Wallis boy brought on Viv's condition. But Mister Geist can't 'ford to lose her. Not in his line of work."

"Do you know when they'll return?"

"Not till next month's end." She blinks drowsily through the dusk. "Who are you, anyhow?"

"Mr. Geist's niece," I improvise. "And I suppose that it's very lucky I was given a spare house key." I pretend to rummage for it in my purse. The housekeeper tires of watching me. "Chance of rain," she says, a parting warning before she scowls at the gloaming sky and plods back inside.

I wait until I'm sure she's gone. My hand reaches up to disengage a hairpin. Then I crouch and fit the pin, jiggering it. *A spy can open whatever is locked.* I only dare let myself exhale when I feel it click.

Part of me is exalting. *A spirit in turmoil wants to expose a truth,* Geist had said, *or make a confession.* But Will hadn't wanted to make a confession. No, his unfinished business had to do with exposing his brother's betrayal.

The knob turns. I pause a moment. I've never been an intruder.

Darkness makes the furniture unfamiliar and adds to my sense of guilty otherness. I find the matches to light the oil lamp in the front hall. Aware of every creak in the floorboards, I carry it to the sitting room. If Geist had been here, I'd have brandished both my letters in a bittersweet victory. I'd loved Will. It had never been otherwise, despite his brother's steady poisoning of my memories.

Quinn's insinuations and lies had weakened me. Worse, they had eroded my trust in Will's love. But now I'm frightened. Geist is my only confidante, but when I needed him most, he disappeared. Alone as I feel, I must heed his advice as never before.

Any consecrated space, Geist had told me. But not a church.

"And that makes sense," I whisper aloud. Will hadn't ever been much for ceremony. And certainly not Pritchett House, where he'd always escaped whenever he was angry with his brother. Geist's own home is a sanctuary. Devoid of family members and memories, receptive to lost and searching spirits, it's where Will had knocked.

I take care as I enter the sitting room. What faint sound there is comes from the two ticking clocks and my own shallow breath. I sit on the edge of my usual chair across from Geist's, my eyes sweeping the shadows, my hands gripping the seat cushion. Hope is all I've got. *Please, Will.*

That last summer, Will used to watch me when I napped. I was always lazing away honeyed hours after our picnics by the pond. Stretched out and barefoot, my head crooked in the bone of my arm, my breath soft with salted air, and the faraway slap of the water setting the course of my dreams. I'd sleep long and deep. So careless with our time. Blissfully ignorant of how little we had left.

Will would observe me, sketch me, then tease me awake with a blade of grass twirled across my cheek. It's the same sensation that passes through me now, with sun on my skin and a brush across my face as I settle back, relaxing my grip, and open my eyes to find the lamp gone out.

The figure is slouched opposite me in Geist's armchair. I stare. He appears like a photograph slowly developing under my eyes. His shoulders are back, and his chin is tipped; his arms are crossed loose at the chest. A familiar position. He is here.

When I speak his name, his answering gaze on me is suffused in love and sadness. As Will's image takes full hold, his lips part. As if to say something in return. His eyes are tender and know me entirely. Then his hand lifts, reaches out, and sweeps across as if to indicate something…

Later, when I remember and relive and savor this moment, all I can conjure is the memory of my unabashed delight. Exaltation. Here he is, so real I could take his own dear face between my hands.

I hear my thin breath, but when I open my eyes—I hadn't realized they were closed—Will is gone.

"No!" I inhale sharply, jumping to stand. Dumbfounded. But he *was* here. Was he here? If he was, he has slipped from the surface. I'm panicked, shocked by the moment, its power and its brevity. No, no, it's not enough. Not nearly enough, after all that I've been through. After all my efforts in trying to find him.

Something in the room has shifted. A subtle nuance, but the moment dangles, teasing me as I work to solve it.

Of course. Both clocks have stopped.

I must stay calm. Will's presence hums through me like a hymn. When I glance down and see the cat, I jump and scream.

"Psst! Scat!" The animal has been crouched motionless at the foot of my chair all this time. Was that what Will's gesture had indicated?

"Psst!" I hiss again. "Shoo, cat!" It doesn't move—no, it's not a cat, not a living thing at all. It's some sort of object.

And yet…I'm sure it wasn't here when I first came into the room.

I drop to a crouch, and my hands scoop darkness until my fingers swipe the cold metal of the buckle and clasp. Locke's satchel. Yes, that is exactly what it is. I slide closer, unbuckle it, and withdraw its contents. Glass ambrotypes. My fingers count nine in all.

My heart beats with curiosity and fear. In a scramble, I find the box of matches on the mantel, and I relight the lamp.

"All right, William," I whisper. "I know that that you're here and that you've summoned me. Now. What do you want me to see?"

The light is dim illumination. I unknot my dark shawl and drape it over the back of the armchair. Then I arrange the table lamp to shine directly in front. I prop up the first image.

It is a drummer boy, not more than ten years old. An innocent. In a different dress he could be one of Geist's cherubs. I set the plate down and set another against the dark fabric. Here is a colonel or possibly a general, all bristling epaulets and waxed mustache.

Something has changed. The room has gone so cold my teeth chatter. My urge to leave this room is so violent it almost overwhelms me. I'm not sure I can reckon with the truth I might uncover here. But the motions of my body do not listen, and stay mechanical, working smoothly, capably. I exchange the general's image for another. Fallen soldiers, sprawled in the long grass. It twists my heart. The Wilderness, perhaps? It could be any of the countless, unnamed battles.

In the end, what does the name or the place of death even matter?

The next image shows a line of young men. Six in all, but I recognize two. At one end, sitting on the ground, Nate Dearborn. Standing over him is a short, square man with a slack and bearded jaw and a bristle of dark hair, holding the defiant stance of the leader. Is this Curtis? Must be.

And there, second from the opposite end, is Quinn. His shoulders defiant, a tourniquet wrapped around his eye. I don't need the identifying caption at the bottom of the plate to know that I'm looking into the eyes of the Raiders. All dead now, all but one. And William Pritchett is not among them.

On closer inspection, I see the date scratched in the bottom. July 10, 1864.

28.

I stumble from Geist's. I have no money for a hackney, and the local trains have stopped running. All I've got are my own two feet, and the distance is long. It's dark now, besides, and the night is further obscured by an icy spitting rain. Few travelers or carriages take up the road, and none that pass trouble themselves with me.

After one too many stumbles, I break the heels off my shoes as easily as snapping chicken bones. They're ruined anyway, from the muddy gutters. I send the heels sailing into an alley. Good riddance. I'll never wear heels again for the rest of my life.

Soon the roads widen and the spaces between buildings open as I leave the city behind. There are miles of darkness before me. I want to rest, but I push on, hurrying and then slowing to catch my breath before picking up pace again. After a while my legs ache with the desire to stop, and it is only my anxious energy that vaults me forward, onward, charged with no greater impulse than to run.

"Jennie!" The sound of my name slices the night and stops me cold. My skin is a thousand pinpoints of prickling dread. I'd convinced myself to fear neither the dark nor the journey, but his voice is a bullet ripped clean through my body.

Standing in the shadows by the bridge, he has been watching my approach. Waiting for me. I slow.

"Where are you coming from? Why did you leave the house? Jennie, you've missed everything. The entire dinner, even the baked Alaska, which was a splendid sight. By the time I left, they'd moved onto dancing."

"I...had to go."

"Go where? You've been gone for hours." Quinn steps forward. His evening clothes are impeccably tailored to his body. Combed and pressed and clean-shaven, the moon reflects him as exquisitely groomed as I've ever seen. He is the Quinn I used to know.

For a split second I'm sorry I couldn't have witnessed him at tonight's party. It is easy to imagine him presiding at the table. His princely manners, his tapered fingers balancing the stem of his champagne glass as he raised it in toast. I can hear the gale of laughter that would follow one of his reposts. I can feel the flat of his hand on the small of my back as we might have danced, later. The collective flush of all the other girls' envy as I sailed through the night on his arm.

I've come to a standstill. Quinn continues to advance. Courtly, cordially, as if he might request a waltz. "Dearest Fleur, if you'd had any trepidation about this party, you might have given me fair warning. As it was, Mother told the guests you came down with a sick headache."

"I'll have to remember to thank her." My voice sounds girlish and scared.

Quinn stops close enough that I see the glint in his eyes, silver and uncomprehending. The injured eye, almost healed, has taken on an unfixed and cloudy focus. Quinn had once confessed that it hardly diffuses more than light and dark.

Suddenly it is this eye that frightens me most—an eye gone nearly dead that keeps up a pretense of functioning. An eye that stares at me but sees nothing. I jump back as he takes a step forward. A fresh patter of rain blows in on us, briefly blinding.

"But I don't understand. What made you go away? Did one of those absurd Wortleys slight you?"

"No…" I realize I am too scared to speak.

"You can't imagine my frustration to come home and not find you anywhere. Mavis said that when she saw you on the stairs, you looked pretty as a painting. I thought you might be taking a walk around the pond. But your hair, your frock—and what've you done with your beautiful new shoes?" The concern in his voice has an edge of suspicion now.

The entire journey from Boston I'd throbbed with fury and outrage. But the confrontation is not so simple. I am besieged by so many conflicting emotions: apprehension, disgust, exhaustion, anger, fear—and above all, the rush of need to escape Quinn's presence.

"L-let me pass," I stammer, pushing forward, but he blocks me.

"Jennie, what's happened? I've been quite heartsick with worry these past hours. And something is undeniably wrong."

"Let me pass," I repeat. "I'm returning to the house to collect the only thing I've ever cared about. And then I'm leaving."

"Leaving? Why? And why are you looking at me like that?"

It's no use pretending. I square myself in his eye, my voice breaking thin from my lips. "The photograph," I manage. "Locke's photograph, all six of you. Curtis, Dearborn, you…the one you were looking for last week," I add.

Caught off guard, he remains composed. "Yes," he answers simply after a moment. "Yes, you're right. You've found irrefutable evidence—though you know nothing of the context in which that photo was taken."

"Tell me, then."

His voice is even, neither kind nor unfriendly, and his face is inscrutable—his cardplayer's face. "First you tell me this. What prompted you to go running off into the night searching for an item whose very existence you could have known nothing about?"

"When I realized that Will's confession was really yours," I answer. "Your script changed when you began to reuse your left hand. That's what had confused me."

"Your eyes have gone so cold, Jennie. Why do I feel tried and hanged already?"

"Why shouldn't I suspect you?" I cry. "Ever since you came home, you've been polluting me with your lies. You lied to Nate that you and I were engaged. You lied that Will was a dishonorable soldier. You invented his role in a gang of thieves and murderers. You've come back home wearing your brother's skin so that you could steal your brother's life and everything in it. But that wasn't enough for you, because you even wanted to tamp out the honor of his memory. What a low and filthy thing to do. It is beyond reproach, Quinn. It's beyond anything I could have conceived, of you or anyone."

"Certainly, if that's how you wish to see it," he answers me. "Yes, fine, I took on what had been Will's. I did. But only because he would have wanted it that way. For he knew it's what I'd wished for so badly."

"Nate thought it was *you* who'd been hanged," I realize out loud. "He was referring to Will, not you, when he spoke about the 'stuck-up brother.' It never made sense to me that Nate and Will would have been friends—but that's because they weren't. Nate was your friend. What I can't see in this nightmare is *why* Will is not here, and you are."

Quinn stands like a soldier and he delivers his words simply, belying their weight. "I'd written you my last thoughts in that letter. All of it was straight from my heart. I gave that letter to Nate Dearborn, and I told him to find you. I needed for you to know how I felt about you before they killed me." His gaze seems fixed into another time.

"But what about Will? What happened to Will?" I am pleading.

"Enough about Will."

"I won't stop until—"

"—Will is gone and you refuse to believe—"

"—until you allow him the dignity—"

"—Dammit, Jennie, I swear sometimes you nag me worse than Mother."

"But I wouldn't if you didn't act so furtive and guilty, as if you've got—"

"Enough!" His hand whip cracks my cheek.

"Oh!" I reel back, my head snapping against the bridge guardrail as I stumble to my knees. Pain shudders and pings down my neck and arms.

I touch my lips. Blood mingles with rainwater.

Quinn has moved above me, his temper recovered and in check. "What have I done? Forgive me, please, Jennie. I'm not in command of myself. The morphine…and the wine…" Hands on my shoulders, he pulls me up and tries to press me close. A thought grips me cold: perhaps Quinn is insane. I must reason with him carefully.

"I want to know," I say, "so that I might come to my own conclusion."

My blood goes cold at his tone. So reasonable, so pleasant, as if he's worked out every piece of his madman's logic. "My brother was too moral, too sanctimonious and pious for prison. He was unable to do what was necessary to survive, to *thrive*. He threatened to turn us all in…I had to do it if I were to stay alive and get out. To come home to you."

My image of Will at the poker table, free and insouciant, mists away. Now I see brothers arguing over crimes, a locket lost, a girl back home. "Had to do what?"

"We fought. I didn't mean to. But I was angry, he was angry, we hadn't slept in days, hadn't had a warm meal or proper bed…I can't say who started it. I was in a fury—how dare he preach morality? How dare he call us traitors? We just wanted to survive. To survive that hell."

"What happened?" My voice is a whisper.

"He lunged at me, pulled a knife on me. I hadn't meant to finish him, but he'd gouged my eye and I couldn't see, I couldn't think, not in the moment. My hands around his neck did more damage than I expected. So there, I've said it. In war, Fleur, we are not in our right minds…" Quinn's fingers are trembling slightly as they brush my bloodied lip.

I shake him off. The rain is sloshing on my skin and inside my head. "You killed him." My nightmares, the strangling—Will had been warning me. It is all so stunningly, horrifically clear. I step back. "You killed your own brother."

"You're exhausted right now. You're hearing this story but not the nuances of it. Tomorrow you'll feel differently. Truly, you could learn to love me. We'd purchase ourselves an entirely new and better life. We'll refurbish Pritchett House exactly to your liking, for there'll be plenty of money just as soon as we're married."

"Plenty of money as soon as we're married…" I repeat softly.
He flinches.

"Quinn? What do you mean?" I press. "Do I have money? Of my own?"

"You do have some, yes," he answers. "A tiny bit that's coming to you when you turn eighteen. Father is the executor of your trust, and he didn't think you needed to know, or you'd start grasping for it. But it could be drawn if we were wed, as I'm of legal age."

"This is the first I've heard of a trust."

"What does it matter? Mine would become yours, yours would become mine. As it happens with any husband and wife."

The blow to my head is taking its toll. I blink, dizzy, my knees seem to lack strength, my vision blurs.

My own money. A "tiny bit." Yet significant enough that nobody has ever confided it to me.

It is too much deception, all at once. I'm all out of fight. I lean back against the struts of the bridge, as far away as I can get from Quinn without inciting him.

"Jennie, it's not a queen's ransom, believe me. Besides, I'd love you if you didn't have a penny." Quinn closes the space between us. "How can you doubt my love? Think of it this way. It was the luckiest thing in the world—for both of us—that you'd thought Will wrote that stupid confession. On some level of your unconscious mind, I think perhaps you secretly wanted Will to have written it, to absolve me. To put the war behind us and start fresh. With me."

"No, that's madness…" Uttering this word, I am fearful of it, for it seems too apt a description.

Quinn waves me off. He speaks with utter conviction. "I'd assumed you'd gone a bit off anyway. Burying your own necklace, drawing on the windows. I wanted to help you. I still do." His hands grip my shoulders in entreaty. "In time, I'd hoped, you'd grow to love me for it."

The necklace, the heart, the presence in Pritchett House. All along, Will has been trying to warn me. "You were never going to tell the truth," I realize aloud. "You'd have taken this secret of yours to your death."

Quinn's grip intensifies. "You promised we'd be happy again," he says. "You promised."

"With *you*?" I have to laugh. Unwise, I gauge, too late.

"Have you been playing with me all along, then?" Something in him has died, gone empty. His tone is as cold as his eyes. "It makes me wonder, how could you have cared for me at all if you can turn venomous so quickly? I've been a fool." He releases my shoulders to catch my wrists with hands rough as rope. "Suppose it's a mistake we'll both have to live with." He shoves me back, as if shaking out a handkerchief. "Not that yours will be a particularly long life." As my spine slams against the guardrail, fresh pain breaks through my body. "But I'll think of you a little, Fleur. I promise I will."

"You're hurting me!" But he won't stop. "Let's go home," I find myself saying. Pleading. "Where it's warm and dry, and we can talk like sensible beings."

Quiet astonishment passes into his face as he considers this. If there is a moment when he hinges between this suggestion and another action, it is far too short. His brother, ever the rescuer, steadfast in his desire to do right by his loved ones, hadn't realized what he was up against. He had been the same young man right to the end. And the Quinn standing before me now was the same Quinn.

The beast he always was. Determined to have everything he wanted and sure that he was entitled to it.

I have seen him every day since his return. And yet I've not managed to see this.

"No more talking. I'm tired of your tricks, and I won't live a life where you wrangle your stupid secrets over my head." He turns faintly seductive as he caresses the side of my cheek. "You never did learn to swim, did you, Jennie?" He smirks. "Don't worry, love. When you're closer to death, it won't be as painful as you think. In fact, I believe it might be a bit like falling asleep."

"No...you wouldn't..."

"And then you can join them both. Your twin and your beloved."

He will kill me. No doubt about it. He has killed before. And killed and killed. "You don't know what you're doing."

"What I am doing," he responds, dulcet as a choir boy, "is playing the part of your bereaved fiancé. Not a soul will argue that your suicide was caused by heartbreak...after all, you still love my poor, dead brother. You visited that preposterous spiritualist often enough—everyone's borne witness to your endless melancholia. Marrying would have gotten me the money. But so will your death, almost as easily. My father is your next of kin, after all, and he is not as young as he once was. I'll inherit all the same. I'll just have to wait a little longer for my fortune than I expected...or maybe I can speed that along as well."

His grip is squeezing out my breath. My eyes float closed. I can't bear to look into a face that has deceived me so utterly.

"You've figured out everything, haven't you?"

"I'd never planned on loving you, Jennie. I never planned on

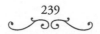

that. It made everything so complicated. And, yes, I do blame you for it. But your spell on me is over, my dear. I've decided I don't want my brother's used goods after all."

Then Quinn dips forward and kisses me, licking the blood from my split lip down to my chin before he pushes me backward over the bridge with such brute intention that I hear the splintering, then the crunch and snap of wooden railing as I lose balance and fall.

29.

My own clothing is my coffin. My heavy hoop wire, the whalebone corset, the layers and layers of underskirts. Pinned and hooked and buttoned to my body, they drag me under. My arms and legs twist in helpless panic as water closes around the crown of my head. I'm sinking, drowning, imprisoned in my cage of finery.

Swim. The word terrifies me. Once I saw an old man's body washed into harbor. His bloated flesh and lips blue as meat have held in my memory ever since and are what I see in my mind's wild eye. My legs and arms flail; my skirts billow up over my face.

As if it is being tugged by invisible fingers, I feel my ring loosen from my finger. I open my eyes and watch it drop, a chunk of red and gold light through black water, and then out of sight. So this is my death.

Any consecrated space. The ruined sketches, the stain of ink. Will had wanted me to remember his fury. That afternoon had been the angriest I'd ever seen him. He'd come to me in rage, not guilt. Betrayed by a brother who, in the end, had been a stranger to him. A stranger to us both. A murderer to us both. Will's fate is now mine.

Water is heavy like sand, and it is pushing me deeper. I'm

insignificant as a pebble down a well. My death will be silent. No screams, no wailing witnesses, no grip of hands hauling me to safety.

I imagine Quinn leaning over the rails, the moon catching the reflection in his dead wolf's eye. His hands loose in his pockets as he turns away from me, just as he'd turned away from his brother. His mind carefully, detachedly preparing his alibi.

Quinn is doubtless correct, in every word, about how my death will be perceived. *Alas, poor Jennie, she never did move past her grief—perhaps it is all for the best.*

Maybe they're right. What use is my life if I've been wrenched from everyone who meant most to me? I have lost so much. Love made me mad with pleasure, but loss has made me mad with grief. What a pleasant sleep my death will bring. Unplagued by nightmares or grim reawakening.

But this is not the way it will be. For he is here, as he always has been. Pressing colder, pressing upward. I can't perceive, I can't touch, I can only sense the overriding force of his protection and love. Enormous and quick and unexpected, it lifts me sharp under my arms as if I'm being offered to heaven itself. Forced up against the current, I rise in a rush of vertigo.

A spy must...A spy must...

I open my mouth to cry out, and water rushes in to fill the scream. My story is not over, and today is not my death day after all. I break through the surface of the water, gasping and reborn.

# 30.

A ghost will find his way home. But I am not a ghost. And this house is not my home.

My feet are frozen and blistered and bare. I hardly feel the pinching pain of the gravel. My hand on the front door is a muddied bird claw. My sodden skirts drag along the carpet runner, then the polished parquet floor, as I tread steady, a sleepwalker, down the familiar hallway and into the drawing room, which overspills its gilded jewel box of assembled guests.

After so many hours in the dark and pouring rain, all this heat and light, the spiced and fruited perfumes and powders, the voices richly lacquered in wine and laughter, seem to wrap over me in a bracing clench of humanity.

Their awareness is gradual. And then I am the entire performance. All jaws drop mid-gape. All eyes round. Fingers lift to press over mouths and chins.

Scandalized murmuring, whispering, but ultimately silence becomes the disease, spreading through the room and infecting everyone. Oh, but I am a sight worth seeing. I find the full specter of myself in the mirror above the mantel. My face is ghoulish, as deadly as the Du Keating girl. My eyes are fear-gored, my skin is scraped to blood. My hair has fallen from its pins to hang in a dripping shroud. Mud and scum streak black marks over my neck and arms.

And in my own expression, I see my beloved. That hot August day. Will's face twisted in fury. His sketches wet and streaming, ruined. As angry as I'd ever seen him. It is the core of that rage that shoots through the ether, a jolt of his life energy pumping through my own outraged blood.

"You'll be true to me forever?" he'd asked me once, almost with anger. No, not anger. Passion.

"Always and forever," I'd answered. "With my whole, entire heart."

In the mirror I am one of Will's ruined sketches. And yet I have survived. I have lived to avenge the betrayed, to damn the culprit.

I've sensed him from the moment of my entrance. Moments before he became aware of me. There is something in the way Quinn stands. Perhaps it is the angle of his head, or maybe it's just the luck of an opportune moment, cozied into a corner and basking in Aunt's attention. How could I never have seen it? That inexorable devotion, that primal and insistent blood tie between a mother and her only son?

Who was I to ever think I could come between them?

Who was I to them?

"Careless, careless. I suppose you were anxious to get back to playing host." My words are to Quinn, and my voice carries through the room, a clarion call for everyone to hear. "But such sloppy work, Quinn. You ought to have held my head under the water for three minutes. Or checked my pulse to make sure it had stopped."

"Fleur, darling," says Quinn, forcing a smile as he stands and steps away from Aunt. I can see and smell his fear. It is palpable to me, no matter how intently he tries to look both unconcerned and dutiful. "You're not well. Come, I'll take you up to your rooms myself."

"How very kind of you. But unnecessary." My gaze flicks to Uncle Henry. "Am I to presume that the bill for this party you cannot afford will be subtracted from my trust?"

Uncle looks so startled and abjectly shamed that I want to laugh. Good. Let him crumble. Let him be the talk of Brookline, of Boston. Let his worst nightmare of public scandal come true.

"Jennie, I must insist." Quinn, ever the actor, signals to Doctor Perkins, who half stands despite being pink with drink. Quinn knots his hands together while furrowing his brow, trying to look helpful, though his good eye has a cast of madness to it. "Sir, my apologies. I ought to have engaged you sooner," he says, "for I'm afraid that our dear Jennie has been very ill."

"If I am sick, it is only with disgust." I speak quietly, but the silence in the room picks up my every syllable.

The Wortley sisters, tucked into a far corner of the drawing room, are stupefied. Finally they are eyewitnesses to the event of the season. How it will be gnashed on and licked up in parlors and sitting rooms all over Brookline and beyond.

But none of this interests me.

"I can only stay a minute." I steel my eyes to Quinn's. Every ear listens for what I am going to say. "I'm here to collect Mavis. And then I must go."

"But...what has happened?" Aunt Clara blinks at me as though seeing me for the first time. Her eyes are wide and childlike. So overwhelmed, she cannot take any ownership, not just yet, of what in days and weeks to come she will recall in horrific detail and brutal shame. Thankfully, she will have plenty of time to reexamine every moment from the self-imposed exile of her boudoir.

But now all she can do is blink, her voice piping with feigned, girlish innocence. "What...what has happened to you?"

"I am alive," I say simply. "That's all."

And that's enough. The night is over, but my own journey has only just started.

DALLMEYER LENSES AND APPARATUS

THIS APPARATUS is useful for all kinds of work, Instantaneous pictures of moving objects, Portraits, Groups, Landscapes, Architectural and Engineering Subjects, etc. The Lens is of a most rapid type and has a patent Instantaneous Shutter working with the greatest rapidity, also our patent Adjustable Diaphragms showing at a glance the precise aperture by a divided scale, and the relative times of exposure with different apertures. The Camera is beautifully made and folds up into the smallest compass possible. The Tail Board opens out of Camera and the Lens Front slides out and clamps. Fine Adjustment is obtained by Rackwork. The bellows are made of leather, and the whole apparatus of which, over 15,000 have been sold, is pronounced the *sine qua non* of the Amateur Photographer.

LENS: f10, Dallmeyer Triple Achromat, Waterhouse stops.
Sold by Watson. SERIAL NO. 9114 (1865).
CONSTRUCTION: Spanish mahogany with brass binding
& brass fittings, red leather bellows. Dovetail joints.
FORMAT: 8" x 5" wet-collodion plates held in slides.

EPILOGUE

Mavis didn't come with me that night as I'd hoped. Rarely does life work out so smoothly. I took the cat instead. Mavis endured another fifteen thankless months at Pritchett House before breaking free one crisp November afternoon in a storm of tears and a full season of unpaid labor to arrive last week at my modest doorstep.

This is good timing. For I am eighteen years old now and newly landed in the bed of my inheritance. Or at least my worth is enough to move from Madame's Broussard's upstairs spare room into tasteful apartments of my own on Beacon Hill. And I have the space and money to keep Mavis, for which I am grateful. But I will continue to supplement my income doing fine lacework for Madame, even though sitting for so long drives me to distraction, not to mention the strain it puts on my eyes. It's an honest living, and Madame and I enjoy a cordial relationship. We're busy, too. Now that the war is over, the city wants to heal. It is taking down its crepe, bravely lifting its chin, and starting to feather itself with new money.

I'd heard the gossip, but it is Mavis who brings me the first official news of Pritchett House. "Miss Jennie, I have left that house a ghost of itself" is how she describes it.

I'm not surprised. I've always thought of it that way. Apparently, Aunt has not spent another penny on its upkeep. Mavis says that the roof won't last another winter. "It's a nightmare, Miss. There's mice in the piano seat cushion, and water stains on the ceiling in the dining room, and more chips than china in the tea set."

According to Mavis, Aunt herself ventures out only for church and the occasional Boston Ladies' Aid function. She is too shamed, too poor, too wrecked to do much more. I highly doubt Brookline society mourns her absence any more than they celebrated her presence.

Uncle Henry is much the same, but I knew that, too. He still trundles back and forth from Boston regularly—once I passed him on Fulton Street and he stared right through me, though his cheeks purpled and he immediately took out his waistcoat watch to study. No matter. We have nothing to say to each other.

Finally, Mavis brings news of Quinn, who has yet to take a position at his father's bank. His retreat has been utter and absolute. A hermit prone to midnight walks and endless card games where he is the only player. Last winter he reconfigured all of the gardens himself, hauling down shrubbery in the dead of night and uprooting Aunt's plantings.

"But he refuses to chop down that dratted butternut tree," Mavis tells me. "'Spite that lightning split it in two last summer, and the wood is mostly dead and rotting. Many's the evening I'd look out the window to see him sitting beneath it, gazing out at nothing." She shivers. "Oh, but he's a haunted man, for sure. The day girls never stay—hardly nobody has nothing to do with him, save that silly Miss Wortley."

Quinn doesn't have to live this way. It's common knowledge that he'd only have to clap his hands and he could be betrothed to

Flora Wortley, thus ending any Pritchett financial woes. Mavis tells me that poor Flora calls every other Tuesday, her ringlets plump as pickles, her hopes as exposed as her décolletage. "Mister Pritchett is always courtly," Mavis reports, "but he never shows any particular interest in her bosom or her bank account."

Strange what we are capable of, and what we balk on.

Quinn might not have peace, but I've got mine. Will led me to the truth. Once that truth was known, he let me go. In the same spirit, Toby has receded to the burnish of my fondest memories. I wear my locket, and I keep their photographs beside my bed, but time is fading the tonal papers to ever lighter shades of gray and brown. It's a natural process and inevitable. Both boys had delighted in the joy of life. For me to fall into grief would not have pleased either of them.

So I try not to dwell on what I have lost as I take my place in the to and fro of city life. But in the art of photography I have yoked my present to my past. For my last birthday I bought myself a Dallmeyer, shipped all the way from London. My parlor doubles as a studio, where I fashion simple images—certainly no phantom spirits. Rather, I pay local children to pose for *tableaux vivants*, or re-creations of poetic works, or studies in truth and beauty.

The years will tell if I have any talent. Foremost, a photographer needs a teacher. Which is why I've brought some plates to Geist today.

"Miss Lovell." He greets me as amiably as ever.

Viviette's greeting is more reserved, but I know she'll have tea and fresh Irish scones waiting—an improvement on Geist's stale sandwiches of last year. The birth of little Seamus—and maybe her new position as lady of the house—has set her mind at ease and clears her to do what she does best.

"A lovely day," I mention as I hand Geist my plates and follow him into the sitting room. He will look at my efforts later. Right now there is other business to attend to. It had been Viviette's suggestion when she'd run into me earlier this morning at the fish market. Viviette is a woman of few words, but when she speaks, I have learned, it's always wise to listen.

The day is sunless. A cold, shy wind rattles the dying leaves. It's a perfect day for a séance. If anyone can find a passage over to the other side, it is Viviette.

And if anyone can follow her there, it is I.

As we sit at the table, her hand grips mine, soft but tight.

I feel the surge—of her power, maybe. Or my own anticipation. I want so badly to believe that I'm already halfway there.

Geist smiles and tucks his chin to his chest. His own faith is absolute. "Let us begin."

✣ NOTES, ILLUSTRATIONS, ✣
✣ AND ACKNOWLEDGMENTS ✣

Jennie's story has one foot in pure fiction and the other firmly planted in historical fact. We really had so little to fabricate ourselves—bits of history, when needed, just seemed to fall neatly into place.

By the autumn of 1864, when our story takes place, the American Civil War had been going strong for three years. Lincoln had issued his Emancipation Proclamation, the battle at Gettysburg had been waged with enormous casualties on both sides, and Ulysses S. Grant was commander of the Union Army. And yet some of the war's most vicious battles had yet to be fought.

Will and Quinn Pritchett, Tobias Lovell, and Nate Dearborn all helped comprise the Twenty-eighth Massachusetts Infantry. Also known as one of four "Irish Brigades," the Twenty-eighth enlisted soldiers hailed from a variety of backgrounds, including Canadian and other non-U.S. citizens, newer recruits who were mustered in the last years of the war. The boys of the Twenty-eighth fought the Union Army's major battles of the eastern theater; Antietam, Gettysburg, and of course, the Wilderness. Collected in the National Park Service Archive is proof of prisoners from the Twenty-eighth who had been captured in the Wilderness and brought to Andersonville to serve their sentences.

Andersonville, also known as Camp Sumter, was a Confederate prisoner of war camp in Georgia. Built in 1864 to house the spill-over of Union prisoners captured by the Confederate Army, it saw more than 45,000 men pass through its gates. Of these, thirty per-cent never made it out. Overcrowded, rife with disease, and lack-ing adequate food and shelter, Andersonville became an infamous symbol of cruelty and death. The jailers were not only to blame, as the imprisoned themselves often had a hand in their own downfall. Most notoriously, a group of prisoners known as the "Andersonville Raiders" terrorized fellow inmates with theft and murder. Hunted down and rounded up, the ringleaders were summarily executed, while other suspected Raiders were beaten to death by their peers in an attempt to serve "justice."

The death and despair brought on by the Civil War eventually gave rise to the Spiritualist movement. Spiritualism was a religious ideology popular from the mid-nineteenth through the beginning of the twentieth century. Its followers believed not only that people lived on after death, but could be contacted with the help of "medi-ums": people who were unusually sensitive to communication with the spirit world. Spiritualists believed in a progressive ideology, and those who followed Spiritualist teachings were more than likely to be abolitionists, suffragists, and labor reformers. Spiritualism was not relegated to society's fringes: figures as respectable as the First Lady, Mary Todd Lincoln, had partaken in séance circles, desperate to communicate with her deceased beloved. As the war progressed and casualties mounted on the battlefield, increasing numbers of the bereaved became obsessed with contacting the dead.

During this same time, people on both sides of the Atlantic were developing a new way of recording one's experience of the visual world. Photography, still a new technology at the time of our story, was becoming more accessible and cheap enough to be consumed by the masses. By the late 1850s, albumen prints on photographic paper were supplanting the more expensive and labor-intensive daguerreotypes and ambrotypes, which were printed on glass and metal. *Cartes de visite*, photographic prints mounted on small cards, were inexpensive and easily reproduced. Uniformed Civil War soldiers ordered *cdv* portraits to send back home to their families, while sweethearts and family members sent their own pictures to the soldiers in the field as mementos. Photographs also played a part in bringing home the horrors of the battlefield. This would be the first time that a war would be so realistically paraded in front of civilian eyes.

In the early 1860s, a Boston photographer named William Mumler began to produce visual evidence of ghostly presences. A typical "spirit photograph" consisted of a sharply detailed portrait of a living person with a spectral figure "floating" in the background. Occasionally, one could make out a transparent white arm or a piece of gauzy clothing draped over the shoulder of the sitter. Some spirits looked like photographs; others seemed to be oil paintings. To modern eyes, these photographs appear to be nothing more than double exposures. But nineteenth century viewers were so frightened and convinced of the supernatural images that truth-seekers forced Mumler to trial, where he had to explain in a court of law the science behind his process.

Our illustrated "photographs" are based on old daguerreotypes and albumen prints, most of them of anonymous sitters. We found them in the Online Prints and Photographs Reading Room of the Library of Congress, copied them, altered them, and made them our own. The background patterns are based on actual Victorian designs. Other pieces of Jennie's scrapbook had their origins in the New York Public Library's online Digital Gallery and in the online image archives of the Brookline, Massachusetts Historical Society. We are deeply indebted to an excellent video that clearly demonstrates the nineteenth century photographic processes, part of the online video gallery of the J. Paul Getty Museum.

The illustrations were done with Adobe Illustrator CS3 and a little old-fashioned pen and ink.

We would like to thank our agent, Charlotte Sheedy for her preternatural foresight in throwing us together, and her stalwart colleague, Meredith Kaffel, for all her additional assistance along the way. Thank you to our editor, Kelly Barrales-Saylor, for loving this book as much as we do, and to our families for putting up with our abiding obsession with the ghostly past.

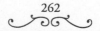

ADELE GRIFFIN has written a number of novels for middle grade and young adult readers, including the Witch Twins and Vampire Island series, as well as the novels *Sons of Liberty* and *Where I Want to Be*, both National Book Award Finalists. She lives with her husband and daughter in Brooklyn, New York.

LISA BROWN is the illustrator and/or author of nine books, including *How to Be, The Latke Who Couldn't Stop Screaming,* and *Baby, Mix Me a Drink.* She draws the Three Panel Book Review cartoon for the book section of the *San Francisco Chronicle.* She lives in San Francisco with her son and her husband, who is rumored to be Lemony Snicket.

A ghost will find his way home. But I am not a ghost.
And this house is not my home.

After losing her parents and her brother, falling in
love with Will was Jennie Lovell's last opportunity for
happiness. But then she lost him too . . .

As Jennie tries to mend the pieces of her broken
life, she feels an eerie presence from something
otherworldly . . . something that won't let her leave
the past behind.

Acclaimed author Adele Griffin
and bestselling illustrator Lisa Brown
have created a spellbinding mystery
where the living cannot always be trusted,
and death is not always the end.

Guided Reading Level: Z
Lexile®: 800L

www.scholastic.com

ISBN 978-0-545-34349-7

$6.99 US
50699

EAN

9 780545 343497